all these things

something of a memoir

Praise for *All These Things*:

all these things

something of a memoir

◆ ◆ ◆

TYLER REEDUS

SYNCLECTIC MEDIA

Published by **Synclectic Media**
Seattle, Washington
www.synclectic.com

Publisher's Cataloging-in-Publication Data

Reedus, Tyler
  All These Things: something of a memoir / Tyler Reedus. – 1st ed.
  p. cm. –
  Summary: Life as the most available loser is something Sam Reed is no stranger to. As he tries to come to terms with himself and the world around him, he faces tough decisions about life, religion, depression, and constant struggles with his ADHD and his sexuality. Can Sam pull himself out of the rain and see the best life has to offer? Or will he fall victim to the pressures of the influences that surround him and his friends?

  Library of Congress Control Number: 2011941480
  ISBN: 9780615557830
  [1. Gay—Fiction. 2. Coming of Age—Fiction.] I. Title.
[Fic]—813.6R   P-CIP

10 9 8 7 6 5 4 3 2 1

Ω
First Edition
Printed in the United States

This book is dedicated to anyone who fights the idea of conformity. To those who refuse to compromise who they are for what other people want them to be. To those who have been told they weren't smart enough or good enough to succeed. To all people out there whose race, religion, sexual orientation, gender, or appearance has made them feel inadequate or defeated. To everyone who is still in this darkness of not seeing a way out of the hurt,
I promise you this:

It gets better!
Don't give up.

10% of the publisher's proceeds from
All These Things will be donated to
It Gets Better Project.
www.itgetsbetter.org

Author's Note

I would like to take this moment to extend my deepest gratitude to all who stood by me and encouraged me to not only tackle this project but to actually finish it. To the people who not only provided the physical tools to assemble this book, but the emotional tools to stay with it and keep moving both myself and this project forward, I thank you. There are many remarkable souls who have contributed their time and friendship to make me the person I am today; you know who you are and I love you so very much. The dream has finally come true and it would not have been possible without you.

I extend a special thanks to four very dear friends in particular for their help in remembering facts and with the development of some of the stories you're going to read in here. They are: Jody Dykstra, Courtney Shadbolt, Alex Berry and Nicole Redmond.

I would also like to thank my beautiful mother Jackie, for helping me recall those childhood memories that my mind had unwillingly left in the past. Even when I knew better, you always knew best, didn't you? I love you so much Mom.

It should be said that I was very young when some of the events in this book took place and as a result of this I had to title "All These Things" as "something of a memoir" because even though what you are about to read is based on true events, I have had to tell some of the stories in this book with little fact and all imagination. I promise, however, that I was as fastidious as I could be and every dream and recollection, down to almost every detail to my retained memory is as close to what happened as I could get it. I feel like my life has been such a story so far and that the lines between fact and fiction have been so blatantly smudged as is it, that, as a writer and natural storyteller, it would seem silly to try and not make this into some sort of a production.

Of course all names in this book (which most are references to songs by the band The Killers, another group of people deserving of my gratitude) have been changed or kept confidential for a reason. The people I know, including myself, are such characters anyway. Any similarities you may find with this book and any other are purely coincidental and I assure you everything read here lives rightfully within the author's imagination and in his past. If you see a blatant error, then I apologize. It's mine.

With all this being said ladies and gentlemen, I hope you enjoy your stay.

An Important Preface

When I told people I was writing a memoir of my life, the statement that I heard the most (to no surprise of mine) was "Already? But you're so young!" Yes, it's true, I'm only twenty-three years old and already I'm telling you about the events of my life thus far. I have to be honest with you, this really all started as a kind of therapy for me. I wanted to have all of my stories down where I could read them and see them everyday instead of trying to harbor all these different events inside. Well certain stories started going deeper and then began to tie together and before I knew it, I was writing a book that I had never even intended to publish.

When you really look at some of these stories, they aren't even that excruciatingly remarkable. Just a little out of the realm of what some might consider those led by a 'normal' child. I don't know what it's like to be homeless,

I've never been addicted to hard drugs, and I don't think I've ever been shot at, which probably would have made for an extra spicy kick, but, let's be real for a minute; not a whole lot of people know what *any* of those feel like. I do, however, know what it's like to feel alone and sad, to want to belong to a part of something bigger, to feel like I don't belong and that I'd always be considered an outcast. Feelings that are all, for the most part anyway, pretty universal. I don't think I could name a single person who hasn't felt like they were the only ones on Earth at one point or another and that's what I want you, reader, to have. Not something unrealistic, something relatable. I feel as though there are too many people that are my age, maybe even younger, possibly older, who feel as though they are the only ones like them and not in the sense of individuality. For the good majority of time that I have spent alive, I have always had this feeling that I am a wounded fish in a sea full of hungry sharks and for anyone else feeling the same way I want this to be a tool you can turn to. I want my voice to be able to say to you, "I know, I've been there, I'm here now. Let's do this together."

My favorite literary work now for the past seven years, since my discovery of it around 2004, has been Stephen King's romantic nightmare "Misery" which has been a key inspiration and sturdy frame for how I have written my own book. I remember reading it in a matter of about three days and being enchanted by its eerie elegance, attractive speech, and hauntingly unforgettable protagonist Annie Wilkes who holds famed writer Paul Sheldon captive after rescuing him from a car accident and after finding he kills off the main character in the book series she's been so obsessively entangled with, keeps him prisoner in her house and makes him write another book bringing her back to life. At first, that's all I saw. A man trapped by a psychotic woman. It wasn't until I saw an interview with King that the true meaning struck home. King explained that Wilkes was a metaphor for not only the book that Sheldon was writing, but for every writer and their work in the sense that what we write can seem to torture and haunt us—even punish us if we write something that is in one way or another unworthy of us. Annie was the book and Paul's purpose remained unchanged, he was the prisoner to that book. We all have something that's haunting us, we all have an Annie Wilkes, and sometimes in order to move forward we need to burn our books, (burn our Annies) and only then can we move forward with what will truly propel us as writers.

After finishing "Misery" I felt like I had been both kicked in the balls and had a burning void filled at last with a contented wholeness, like a satisfied hunger or a fully charged battery. It was the greatest feeling I could have ever asked for from a book and I cannot describe it in words. I hoped one day I myself would be able to write something that would have a similar effect on the audience it was presented to, and I'm hoping that this is going to be it. I wish to hobble your conceptions of both me and the world I live in.

With that being said, about a month before I finished this little project, I had a dream that I feel I must share with you in order for you to experience what was going through my mind when I wrote some of this. I was walking down a street somewhere in my town and it was daytime. I cannot recall what I was wearing but I know I had a crown of thorns on the top of my head. I saw a woman approaching me. She was in her 40's, generously bestowed around the middle, and she was naked. In her hand was a leash which held two children crawling on the ground like dogs, they too, without clothes. I tried to look the other way but she caught my brief stare and hustled towards me. She had my published book in her hand. Furious for whatever reason she asked me if I was the author of this book and I honestly replied that, yes, I was. She looked me in the eye and told me with a fury I had not yet experienced, "I hope you know what you've done." With that, she threw the book on the ground and it burst into flames. She rushed off, one of her children crying, the other applauding me. I woke up shortly after, partly confused but feeling more malaise than anything. The dream passed a personal threshold of being something fantastical and became very real to me and I tried to spend days figuring out what it meant but found it all to be very confusing and put it on the back burner of my mind and went on with just writing the book. It wasn't until a week later when I overheard a conversation take place on the city bus that the dream's interpretation really struck me. It seems to me like the world is being fed filtered non-fiction. Someone will try to write an account of their life but the big time companies will put their makeup on it and strip it of its reality without a second thought because of what might be considered offensive to everyone else. The children on the chain represented those oppressed from being offered the truth while the woman with the leash, fat with selfishness, wanted nothing but to destroy the truth. The reason for the crown is still up in the air, perhaps I will be considered a king among men for writing a book that will, in my hopes anyway, change a pre-conceived notion or perhaps inspire a new idea in the minds of the people. Or it could be that this book will be my crucifixion and after its publication and review from the world, I will have what I call my "Michael Powell" moment and never be allowed to write another book. (For those of you who don't know who British director Michael Powell is, watch the movie 'Peeping Tom' (1960) and you'll know what I mean) But it is my hope at least to continue writing more works after this despite the lurid subject matter that I have chosen to write about.

My vision is this: to pass the hope to you, reader, that in these pages you find your sense of solitude gone and discover a newly gained perspective on the brightness and wonder life has to offer despite the 'sins' that you think you have committed. As for the moral of the story, well, that's really up to you isn't it? I can't go around giving that away. That'd just be too easy. But I will be here to help, to hold your hand if you need to or step back if you need some thinking space. This book is full of hardships, but if you are wise, you already know that the things that beat us down are the ones that make us stronger. I hope I can help you become stronger with the words written in here. For now, cuddle up to me (I don't bite, unless you're into that) and let me tell you a little bit about myself. Just remember that I've been through this; you've got nothing to fear.

Moving onward, E.E. Cummings wrote a poem titled "Pity this monster, man unkind" and in that poem wrote these words..."listen; there's a hell of a universe next door; let's go!" I say we should take this fine advice. You're ready now? Alright, follow me!

Part I:
Beginning & The Available Loser

Beginning: (n.) The time when something begins or is begun. The first part.

Man is least himself when he talks in his own person.
Give him a mask and he will tell you the truth.
   -Oscar Wilde

Lights! Turn on the sound effects! Action! Drop it, drop it on 'em! Drop it on them!!!
   -Pink Floyd, *"In the Flesh?"*

April 1989: Storm

Rain.

That's what there always was, always.

It was there, then it was not, and then it was again.

Juliet was drifting in and out of the rain, hearing it but not quite acknowledging it—almost as if she were telling the weather that she had neither the time nor the interest for it. Trembling slightly, she sat stoic but not emotionless as noises came and went. Footstep after unsynchronized footstep proceeded down the hallway and back again into the bedroom where she lay. The rain was still putting forth its best efforts to make itself known, badgering the glass like a pellet gun with all it had but it was nothing that was going to be getting the attention of Juliet Reed, who, at the moment had a storm of her own to deal with. Most folks around these parts did as well and it was not that Juliet was more prone to tragedy one way or another, but in this instance her storm was not of the traditional wind and rain sort. Juliet was smack dab in the middle of one heck of a maelstrom, and even though she had managed to take surprisingly solid refuge, such shelter had proven to do her little good. The storm came anyway and it was slowly tearing away almost everything she owned. It was incontestable that this thing wanted Juliet desecrated, devastated, and undeniably dead inside. It was a rather curious and particularly violent sort of storm that came in human form, or better yet, a particular breed of darkness that likened itself to human form; a figure known as "Drunken Man," who came and went as he pleased in and out of the room. His face was stiffened but loose from all the alcohol as he wobbled, loading up small suitcases full of his stuff. She listened as the man leaned and stumbled in and out of the room carrying more and more stuff to his suitcases, which had spread out over the majority of the floor, and even some on to the bed right next to Juliet. Scattered across the nightstand were cans of beer. Some were crumpled and empty, others partially consumed and some still full and cold from the refrigerator. On the half-empty bed, Juliet was trying to formulate words and ideas that might be able to mend this whole mess but the denial simply wasn't strong enough. All it would cause was more confusion and a drier throat. She would be defeated before she could even begin.

Juliet was a particularly strong soul, born in the late winter of 1956…the kind of girl who punched any bully in the face who stole her swing on the playground, and as a woman, would be the kind to shotgun a can of beer (which she had done) and fix motorcycles (something she had not done but gave the appearance of being able to do). In high school, she was always welcomed as one of the boys and never had a problem finding a date to the prom. Her beauty exceeded any other girl on the block in Virginia where she lived and went to high school, and she was both the envy of every cheerleader on the squad and the love of every boy who suited up and threw a football. Her father had been stationed in the Air Force and they had stationed many places from San Antonio, Texas to Pemberton, New Jersey. Her parents now lived about 3,000 miles away in tiny Lynville, Washington. They had offered several times for Juliet to come and live with them but Juliet had decided to call Virginia Beach, Virginia home now and had married a man from Georgia who taught college Physics. It was her second marriage. This thought snapped Juliet back to that very darkness, as she remembered where she was and why she was.

Rain continued to pummel the ground. Juliet was caught up in the storm, falling down right along side with it.

The poisoned man turned briefly to his wife with no words and muffled noises, mostly moans. He knew apologies were unwelcome and the smell of the alcohol on his breath would hit her before his words could. Nothing was new anyway; all of the excuses were old and molding, rotting away with the rest of him. Drunken Man was someone Juliet had known for many years but not always had he been this saturated with weakness. He used to be good, even great; a bright man, a friend, a son, and the man Juliet had said yes to at the altar where they were married those nine years earlier. Except now, he was choosing to be no husband of hers anymore. He had morphed himself into an unrecognizable fiend, an alcoholic, a misogynist, and a total wreck. Nipping at the old bottle was sure enough to do that to anyone who came in contact with it. Alcohol was the sort of thing which struck you as a friend who would listen to your troubles after a long day. The guy you'd call up when you were all alone knowing he'd say yes, he's available. When you were in the kitchen fixin' him something to drink, he would plunge the knife in your back before you could ask if he wanted room for cream. He slid the knife in so slowly that once you even realized it was in, you were already bleeding to death and on your way to six feet under. Such was the trick it had pulled with Drunken Man.

Juliet felt like a fool, now sitting at the foot of the bed, her hands folded neatly in her lap, her eyes completely dry. She kept her focus, recalling the excuses, as if it were her own personal form of punishment for not having seen what was going on earlier. This was a lie, however, and she knew it as soon as she had thought it. The signs had been there but she had quickly denied them all and continued to believe she loved a man who did not love her in return. Juliet had found over the course of their relationship that it was rather peculiar that the amount he drank was more than one might consider to be normal, or that he frequently avoided responsibility aside from his job as a nuclear medicine technician. He was no doubt one of the most brilliant men she had ever met, but without her permission he was also one of the worst. He had never struck her or physically hurt her in any way, but the verbal abuse he inflicted had been tremendous enough. He constantly lied about anything and everything and Juliet, once again not wanting to admit the mistake she had made by deciding to be with him, believed him. One way or another she found ways to justify just about everything he told her and make it almost seem as if it were her fault instead of his. He had a poor time coping with the smallest amount of stress which is most likely what had led to his excessive drinking. This could easily be blamed on his highly demanding work and she subconsciously allowed him to get away with it. There would be many instances in which she would try to hold back tears when smiling and saying how much she loved him, though deep within her heart of hearts she knew better. It was something that was simply not going to last.

That wall of false happiness that she had labored over was coming down to the ground and there she lay. The fear had been realized and there was no more escaping it.

However, she still had difficulty bringing herself to believe it. To her, this man had turned into nothing more than a liar. Juliet had well accepted Christ into her life just a few years ago and still felt she was new to Christianity. Being in this new found light, she realized now that every man had his demons and alcohol was one such demon that he'd spent too much time with and over the course of a few years it had deteriorated him into a baroque entanglement of bad decisions and failed hopes. The responsibility for him was simply, in his mind anyway, too insurmountable to cope with. The majority of his scarce coherent energy went into two things: working and spending his money on booze, and constantly convincing Juliet of what a terrible man he really was. The reason for this was Drunken Man's desire to remind Juliet that leaving him and his immature patterns of behavior was a very real and existing option. Not wanting to give up hope for the best though, she kept holding on to everything, damaged or not. Through lies and deceit and backstabbing and regret she would not and could not give up on him or anything else for that matter. Giving up just wasn't something Juliet Reed knew how to do.

Drunken Man reached for one of the semi-cold cans of beer on the shelf and without even realizing she had said so, she had.

"Haven't you and those cans done enough damage tonight?" She seemed to be speaking straight through him as if he wasn't even there, and the truth was…he wasn't. Not anymore, he was gone. As gone as gone could be.

"For the love of God, just leave the beer on the shelf and leave." Juliet had always had a knack for keeping a cool equanimity in these sorts of situations and she kept her words certain, precise, and final. Escaping them was not possible, especially with Drunken Man's current state of laughable intoxication.

He thought for a second on a rebuttal that might be good enough, but somewhere inside knowing he would not come up with anything successful, stitched his mouth back up and did as she had said. Deciding that possibly playing the naïve victim here might do the trick, he pondered on that for a second but it would do nothing but worsen an already stressful situation. More stress was something that he smartly aimed to avoid at this moment, and, assuming his impending defeat no matter what, he gathered up all of the suitcases and left, just like that. The noises that accompanied his departure from the house were cold, expected, and absolute; the stumbling down the stairs, the slamming of the door, the ignition of the car, the revving of the engine, and final drive away from his family. Alone she sat, still hurt and confused but knowing that somehow she would have to persevere and be strong for the well being of her, and whatever else he had left her.

Just then, a small sound broke Juliet's focus from her now-fled partner. It was a low cry, faint but audible. It was nothing strange or unfamiliar and she recognized it immediately. It was the innocent fuss of her seven-month-old son, Sam. Juliet promptly made her way down the hall to the room of her son and she could already see his limbs flailing in his crib before she was even halfway across the room and this allowed a faint smile to form by the corners of her mouth. She just stood still staring at him for a second or two before picking him up in her gentle arms as any perfect mother would. An unexpected tear fell from her eye. Sam did not know, nor could he tell physically that his mother was upset, but he himself began to cry, not loudly, but uncomfortably as if he could sense it anyway, aside from her best efforts at concealing her emotions. They would always be just that close.

"There, there Samuel, mamma's here baby…thaaat's it, shhh shhhh nothing to fear." There was no need to lie. There really was nothing to fear anymore. The fear had left with the figure and all was as it should be, but at the same time it wasn't. As Juliet cradled her beloved in her arms, she whispered a phrase that both comforted and bothered her at the same time.

"Everything will be alright."

Would it be though? How could she know this for sure? One way or another, things would even out for the best. At least this is what her faith told her…that little spark of faith that she had held onto so tightly in case of emergencies such as these. Juliet wanted to believe these words so badly, that, looking into the beautiful bug-eyed look of her infant she, for a moment, undeniably did.

The hours made their march and Juliet just sat in the rocking chair beside the crib cradling and trying to rock him back into a deep childlike sleep. After a few more minutes of comfort, he let out a relieved yawn and closed his new hazel eyes. Sam was placed back in his crib and the world was right again.

His world.

A world without rain.

For the time being, he knew no other.

Instantly, Juliet knew three things: Her husband was out of her life for good and wasn't coming back. Her son was alright; sound asleep and free from harm, and this was the beginning of the toughest road she would ever travel on.

As all these things soaked into her mind, the rain broke and their rattling sound upon the glass faded. It's a very funny thing how the universe orchestrates certain events to play out. Through all of the bad decisions she had made in life up to this point, she had still been blessed with a son. A son who would also go through the light and darkness, sometimes it seemed, all at once. Sometimes he would speak the truth, other times he would lie, but the lessons he would end up teaching her would be among the greatest. For right now, though, he slept, knowing no such plans for his life, nor the talents he had; he didn't even know his name yet but someone told Juliet that this little boy was going to be something remarkably different.

The clock signaled 2:00am and Juliet, exhausted emotionally and otherwise, returned to her bedroom and went to sleep.

The next year and a half would be one of her hardest ever. Juliet would be transporting herself between two full time jobs; one as a makeup artist at a department store, and another as the mother she already was. Her life would consist of working until ten on some nights, going to pick up Sam at whatever babysitter she had left him with that day, driving them both back to their large apartment complex, balancing Sam, the briefcase, the baby bag, and her other effects (sometimes in the pouring rain) in high heels no less, to her second story apartment. She would walk amidst guys who were smoking something in the stairwell making their discourteous comments as she would just keep her eyes up, praying that nothing more would happen. Juliet wasn't sure if it was a thick layer of rebellion, unshakeable determination or a combination of both, but this woman was bone-headedly stuck on doing things her way and her way only. Something that had been passed down to Sam though he did not know he had it yet. It took those one and a half years of high heels, babysitters, and sketchy men prowling her up and down while she held her son in her arms for her to realize that alone wasn't a word she could afford to associate with for much longer. One night, she picked up the phone and called her dad to ask if his offer to come and get them was still good.

"On my way," was all he said, and the conversation was over.

Juliet would start her new life there and nowhere else; but before that light could be seen, this darkness would make its mark on her. Sam would just happen to be caught in the crossfire of her (no, of Drunken Man's) decisions, but the little boy continued to sleep.

It would be precisely seven years from that point on before Sam Reed would be introduced to the drug Ritalin for his Attention Deficit Hyperactivity Disorder which he would be diagnosed with at seven. Following that would be a colorful array of other mind-altering substances that would end up doing more harm than good. Christianity and its customs would make its impression upon him at the ripe age of ten. Two years later, words such as retarded, faggot, and freak would be very familiar to this odd boy's ears. Soon after turning eleven, poetry would begin to bud in his eager mind as would casual lying and unhealthy storytelling and he would get used to being alone because of the two. He would have trust issues during the next three years of middle school and would go through events that took him close to hell and back.

Twelve would concretely confirm his homosexuality, but he wouldn't act upon his desire for men for another seven years; he would also deal with social rejection on a frequent basis. He would never kiss a girl while he was in school. At the age of seventeen, he would be a well-cultivated Christian steward and a classic example of a "church boy" teaching Sunday school and involving himself greatly within his church and the chin-turning appeal of the world's sexuality would be right there next to him.

He would have his first sexual experience with another man at nineteen. Finally, by the age of twenty-two, he would become a comfort drinker, sex enthusiast, and a well-established compulsive liar just like the figure that was swerving out on the road in the dark, on his way to nowhere. In the late winter of 2010, at the same age, an event would happen that would finally allow him to recognize the true difference between light, and the illusion of light.

Samuel Reed, without planning it, would become two people. One was the man he wanted to become, with pure aspirations and God-inspired dreams, whose compassion and loyalty were few and far between. He would be the wholesome and reputable person everybody expected him to be.

The other person he would become was someone he wouldn't recognize in the least. It would be the man who sought out any opportunity for flagrant rebellion and knavish sin. He would be the homosexual slut, the careless drinker, the unpardonable liar, the irresponsible thief, and the ever-arrogant demon. Yet in some strange way, he would embrace this half of him, further isolating himself from everything he had been brought up to believe was right; from everything he both thought and knew to be right. He would be the person everybody whispered wickedly about behind closed doors, behind his back and all these things would lead up to a moment that would change him forever.

None of this mattered, however. Not now anyway, not here.

For the moment's time he slept quietly in his mother's arms being the hero.

He *was* the hero.

Her hero.

He had not left her yet, nor would he ever.

There was a white mist on the ground outside, and a dim glow could be seen over the ocean as the sun, still far off, tried to prematurely break the horizon. His mother was fast asleep now. Through all of this confusion and haze, Sam slept peaceful and content, not knowing that there was a man somewhere out there that he would never meet, who had just left him fatherless.

It seemed years went by...

Minutes and seconds could not even survive here, and neither could the rain, just the sun. Its violent rays punched the hot Mojave sand where Sam Reed stood, his face stained with dried spots of his own blood. There were splotches on his face where brief streams of sweat flowed freely, making him glisten in the ever pressing light. Gripping the smooth pearl-handled pistol that hung impatiently in his leather holster, he waited...

And he waited.

"It's all over, Lee Renwick," Sam proclaimed loudly from his dry mouth. "Either the sheriff gets ya' or this here bullet will!"

Shouting this, Sam tried to cover the anxiety in his slightly shaking voice and was trying hard to believe that Lee wouldn't notice it either.

"What's it gonna be, eh?"

Lee just continued to sneer. There was no indication he even felt threatened by this at all. He just continued to stare Sam right in the eye expecting him to collapse and forfeit under his insidious glare. In any normal situation, giving up would have been an option for Sam who could have very easily distracted him by shooting just to the left of him and then running in the other direction as fast as his boots could carry him. This was an instance however that could not be avoided nor forfeited. The cost this time was too valuable to be risked. That price was his fiancée Sadie whom Lee had corralled around the neck with his silver switchblade. One ill move and the blade would tear her before Sam could even blink.

"Well if ya gonna shoot me Reed you better make it one helluva shot!" He laughed contemptibly, mockingly, and easily. "You gotchaself about as gooduva chance at killin' me as I do of letting your blushin' bride-to-be go."

"Sam! Don't do it darling, he'll kill me!" Sadie muffled to her cowboy, but it would do her no good. Lee had her and was ready to take immediate action on Sadie should Sam try any funny business on him. The whole dispute had begun when Lee became jealous that Sadie had chosen Sam over him a few months before. Ever since then, envy and loathing had been bubbling. It finally came to an unfortunate head the day before when Lee had broken into Sadie's place which was the drafty space right above the Buzzard's Neck Tavern where she worked. The blade quivered in Lee's hands, as though his purpose was to show Sam that he'd better not make a move or else.

It seemed like it might be curtains for Sadie.

Sam, fortunately, had come to class prepared.

Without even thinking about a plan in which to weave this tool into, he played the last card he had in his hand. The spur that had fallen off the bottom of his boots when he and Lee had been fist fighting was still in his pocket and quick as a flash he whipped it out and held it in his hands. Throwing it was certainly a game of Russian roulette, one false aim and Sadie could have been just as much of a goner as Lee. He held it in his hand, twiddled with it and for a second the sun caught its glare and hit a window across from Sam's line of vision. It blinded him slightly but it was nothing too...

Light bulb.

He repositioned it in his hands, letting the sun catch it and beaming a blinding stream of light straight into the eyes of Lee Renwick. The distraction was all Sam needed to landslide this duel. In the moment the light refracted and hit Lee's eyes, he let go of Sadie and wobbled sideways, allowing Sam to take full advantage of this faultless situation. He held up his pistol and gave one well-aimed shot—right at the distracted villain's heart. It almost seemed Lee's mortality was still intact until a thick outpour of blood began its decline down his chest, down his legs, and down to the sand where it dried almost instantly. The bullet had succeeded, and so, of course, had Sam Reed.

Lee looked down at his chest just once and then slowly looked up; he dropped his knife to the ground without another word. The rest of his body followed seconds after. Lee Renwick would never have to worry about being distracted or think of whom to kidnap ever again. Alive as ever, after escaping the grasp of Lee Renwick and his blade, Sadie ran into the arms of her handsome, charismatic cowboy, and began kissing him frantically about the face and neck as any eager, newly-saved woman would certainly be prompt to do.

"Sam! Oh Sam! I knew you could do it dahlin', I just knew that you could save me! Oh Sam you're so incredible!" Sadie glorified her lover as her eyes gleamed in the fleeting sunlight. The praises could not have inflated Sam's ego any more and he welcomed each and every one of them with a cheesy grin and a firmness below.

"'Course I did." He spoke in the egotistical yet charming "damn right I did babe" tone of voice that just turned her on even more. "I'd do it a thousand more times too if it meant I could spend the rest of my life with the woman I love the most." The sun was stepping back down over the mountains and as it did so, Sam lowered his mouth towards her inviting lips and kissed her, he kissed her good.

A wet one.

A perfect one.

A wet, perfect kiss; it was the greatest wettest kiss in the history of kisses.

"I love you," he whispered in her soft ears. The response, which followed it, was not the one Sam had expected.

"Watch what you're doing, you stupid kid!" The voice shattered into Sam's head and startled the daydreamer to his senses. His mind soon recognized both the fantasy and the insult. He was not in the middle of the Mojave Desert with a beautiful woman; he was in his second grade classroom sitting next to an incessantly whiny princess.

(...So yeah, a woman, just lacking in the beautiful aspect.)

"S-so-sorry," he stuttered apologetically after realizing the reason for the girl's swift spiteful statement; knocking over a whole container of markers onto her wooden desk that was right next to his. The markers rolled off the desk and individually smacked the carpet floor.

"Retard." Was all she said back to him and she ended it with a disgusted heave of breath.

"Sam," said Mrs. Clayton, his teacher. "Please clean up the mess you made and get back to your work now. I don't want to have to tell you to stay on track one more time today!"

The girl's remark obviously wasn't enough and the teacher felt as though she needed to provide further embarrassment on the poor kid. Sam turned a mortified shade of red and looked down at his trusty pistol, which had somehow transformed into a disappointing goldenrod colored number two pencil with a diminishing pink eraser on top; it was 1995 and Sam was not in a desert, he was in the second grade. The girl gave him the rest of her snobby look and did not even bother holding back sticking out her stubby tongue at him, then resumed highly immersed in her coloring. For Sam, it was the second time that day that he had found himself engrossed in something that wasn't what he was supposed to be working on. He felt childishly humiliated as the rustle of laughter subdued and eyes averted back to his desk. Sam got down on his knees and quietly began picking up the markers off the floor and putting them back in their container.

Life in a classroom was nothing that came easy to Sam, nor was it something that he ever particularly enjoyed. Recently he had been diagnosed with Attention Deficit Hyperactivity Disorder, commonly referred to as ADHD. It was a condition that was easily treatable with the right medication but unluckily for Sam and everyone else around him, he was not currently on any to assist him with the condition, making tasks easy to other students such as focusing on one topic, sitting still for long periods of time, being organized, and even thinking before speaking (which was the one that usually got him into the most trouble) proved very difficult for the enthusiastic seven-year-old boy. It was not that he was slow or retarded; he just saw the world through a different pair of eyes, controlled by a brain that couldn't keep its attention on one thing. It was a very complicated thing to explain but Sam operated something like this:

Imagine you own a company (your body) and in order to import new products (learn new information) you need to use a computer, a very powerful computer (your brain). However, all the wires (synapses) aren't connected correctly and during all this you're on the other line with someone else (the person who is talking to you) and you're rushing to get everything fixed. In your efforts to rewire this computer, you experience minor crashes, glitches, and freezes. By the time you get the system booted and working, the person on the other line hung up on you long ago because they got impatient, but not you. You were so busy trying to fix everything you felt you weren't given enough time with them. You would have to call them back and apologize for the mess and that you needed everything repeated. Sometimes they would, other times they would not. This happened everyday with Sam, whether he wanted it to happen or not. Sam couldn't even order new parts, he had to work with what he had and it was agitating to no extent, and Sam didn't get any sympathy from anybody. No one knew what it was like to have his brain.

Take one look at Samuel Brandon Reed and you could quickly gather that he was a pasty white, slender kid with large hazel eyes and Dumbo ears. Sam would one day grow into these gauche features but for the time being that's exactly what they remained; unreservedly awkward. He had dark brown hair that was parted down the middle and possessed a mind of its own. It was a disheveled and tousled mess that could have easily been mistaken for an animal that just happened to take refuge a top of Sam's head and suddenly died. He had an anorexic look and could expect no generous gifts from the muscle brigade anytime soon. To further enhance this already freakish structure Sam had had the left side of his pectoral muscle deteriorate from a type of flesh eating virus, therefore leaving a sunken valley of scar tissue over protruding ribs and a lonely nipple.

Socially speaking, he had scant skill whatsoever. During recess, other kids spent time playing games that involved friendly social interaction with each other like soccer, tag, or one of their favorite past-times, making fun of Sam in all of his geekish glory. Sam himself spent about half of his recesses alone usually playing with things that couldn't make fun of him, such as sticks, rocks, or dirt. The other half was usually spent inside the classroom writing lines on the whiteboard such as "I will not throw inanimate objects at my classmates."

Classmates—that was a line that made Sam laugh sometimes.

Those kids were in his class but they certainly weren't any mates of his. They had frequently walked back in from recess with him still writing these things on the whiteboard. It was funny; the teacher didn't make any other student write lines on the whiteboard except for Sam. "Oh that's right…if he saw it, he would remember it." That's what his psychiatrist had told him about ADHD minds one time when he and his mom were in for a visit—the objective of the meeting being to explain to Sam what exactly ADHD was and ways in which he could help it but he remembered nothing of the meeting other than that it was raining and the doctor wore a red tie with tacky blue stripes. Medication was brought up, but was quickly shot down as his mother believed him to be too young to be under the influence of such powerful drugs.

He was further scorned for his inability to socialize with everyone else, something he so desperately wished he could, but wasn't anything that he could help. The ability to make friends simply hadn't clicked yet; the ADHD hindered. So for now, they enjoyed making him the butt of ridicule which made him less desirable to be around. This forced him to continue his playtime all by his lonesome. It was a sadistic, never-ending cycle of scholastic degradation.

The teacher he had wasn't a heap of help either being as his ADHD made him difficult to maintain in the classroom. Sam knew that, and consequently, so did his teacher. When punished, they usually used something ill fitting and cruel. Even if he didn't really do anything he was a quick and easy target.

His punishments were daily and usually in some way shape or form very shameful. If Sam couldn't sit still he was strapped to his seat with a seatbelt. If he was talking then he had to stay in for recess and wasn't allowed to speak a word. If the teacher even thought Sam did something wrong, he would be withheld recess or lunchtime in the cafeteria, which given the fact that everyone who hated him ate in the cafeteria, this may not have been so bad. I mean he did everything else on his own so he guessed it was only fitting. Throwing objects at kids, which in Sam's mind was not a crime at all since they were the ones who instigated the torture, would put Sam in the position of writing those lines on the whiteboard repeatedly for the entire recess and sometimes lunch too as well. Calls to his mother while she was at work were increasingly common as well.

"Ms. Reed, yes this is…yes it's your son again. I'm sorry but we just can't handle him today. We're locking him up in the dungeon without any air, food, or interaction for the rest of the day. He's refusing to cooperate and not doing as he is being told so that's just what needs to be done. I just thought I'd interrupt you while you were working and trying to make a meager living to support your family and inform you of how much we do not like having your devilishly rambunctious ball of fail at this school. We'll also have to have him sent to the principal's office in shackles with a referral. Thank you for your time Ms. Reed. I'll be sure to set up a parent teacher conference during your lunch hour very soon so I can express my deep loathing for this thing to your face. Okay well, thank you again and have a great day, buh-bye!"

These were the caustic words Sam was sure he heard every time; even when the teacher was trying to mask the frustration and craziness in her voice, it still sounded like she would burst into hysteria at any moment and start throwing things at him. What made matters worse, to Sam at least, was that most of the time he was unaware that he was even doing anything wrong. Certain days the playtime in the class would be cut short due to a lengthy lesson and Sam, trying as hard as he could to make it a day where he would finally make a good impression, listened and paid attention with all that he had but he was left powerless by the entertainment of a butterfly outside the window, an especially difficult foe to beat. He would begin doodling something on his paper to keep him occupied or engage in one of his favorite pastimes, watching the weather. Sam loved watching the weather. Weather fascinated him, all of it. When he wasn't being anti-social and hating everyone, he was being anti-social and loving everything else around him. The days where he was not in trouble or in high demand of being taunted, he would find a quiet place on the grass…usually far away from the prying eyes of his class "mates" and just watch the sky. Sam knew all the clouds by name and would try to predict what the weather was going to do based on what kinds of clouds he saw. He had a great appreciation for nature and everything in it and he loved learning about all kinds of weather and different animals. He also loved reading. Sometimes when Sam was having trouble concentrating and the teacher wasn't being a total tyrant, she would excuse him to go to the library so that he could sit on the beanbag chairs and read. He would spend minutes looking at a book before the next, obviously more interesting book, caught his eye and then he would move on to that one and work on it for a while instead. As distracted as he was sometimes, he was always eager to learn something new no matter what the subject, except of course for math, his least favorite. Math, along with sitting still and group activities were among the things he disliked the most.

Overall, despite his chemical imbalances, Sam was in fact trying his hardest to be a normal boy with a contagious personality and interests. At times esoteric, he was enjoyable and relatively normal. But to the rest of the world, he was viewed as a freak and an outcast and there was little room in the world for people such as these. It wasn't like he had much of a choice though, he felt as though he would always be the playground's greatest available loser. His acceptance by other kids meant the world to him but inevitably, at too early an age, come to terms with. It was what people were comfortable with and there could be no altering the comfort zones of the superior.

Sam was unmindful to what the teacher was continuing to talk about.

His mind was elsewhere.

His attention was outside, with the weather.

It had started to rain.

So had he.

♦ ♦ ♦

The door slammed shut with an abominable thud that startled Juliet as she turned around from the kitchen just in time to see Sam running up the stairs. She already knew he was crying. It had been the last day of school before winter break started. Juliet stopped what she was doing and, nearly tripping up the stairs to do so, rushed to her son's aid.

"What's the…" was all she managed to get out before Sam lifted his head from his pillow.

"Mommy please don't make me go back there! Please! It's so bad! I don't want to go back there ever again!" he begged of her. This plea would be enough to break any mother's heart. It wasn't to say that Juliet was not concerned, but knowing Sam someone had probably tricked him into believing the light switch in the classroom controlled the sun and Sam had believed them, which of course had caused a riot throughout the entire rest of the room. Sam wasn't mentally challenged but when it came to the subject of the light being on and no one being home, it was indeed a frequent occurrence for him.

"What happened *exactly*?"

"The kids make fun of me so much."

"Well I'm sure Mrs. Clayton can…" again she found herself cut-off by the ranting child.

"Mrs. Clayton does too!"

This changed things. Students tormented Sam daily and this was something he had dealt with not well but as well as could be expected with the occasional small breakdown to his mom but a *teacher* making fun of her son?

"*How* did she make fun of you, Sam?"

"She told me I couldn't sit still if my life depended on it. I know she's right but I'm just…I'm so tired of being a problem child."

Her brow unfurled and a calming smile came across her face, soothing Sam a little. Clearly this was an issue with his ADHD and Juliet was adamant about scheduling an appointment with Dr. Keuning as soon as she possibly could.

"You're not a problem, Sammy. You just need something to help you focus and sit still."

"Like what?"

"I'm gonna make a call to the doctor and see if he can help out. Do you want Teddy?"

He didn't speak but assuredly nodded his head.

Although Sam was a big kid now, at the momentous age of eight he could still not resist the comfort and company of his teddy bear and he held onto it tightly, knowing full well that it was the one thing that would never hurt him. All he could do was make Sam not feel so alone as was the job of every teddy bear. He continued to cry.

No, that wasn't right. He wasn't crying; he was raining.

He was pouring.

The next day, Juliet made him pancakes. Sam was playing with his baseball cards at the table and eating his pancakes at the same time. He was getting the syrup all over his fingers and consequently all over the cards as well so he washed up and put his cards away.

"Sammy, hurry up. We need to leave soon. Put your clothes on so we can go." Getting ready in the morning was usually something that took a while to do for Sam because it was difficult for him to stay focused on what he was doing. A few minutes later Sam came staggered down the stairs with some toys and books for the eternal half hour drive where he would be confined to his mother's white ford Taurus. After quickly grabbing her purse, they got in the car and were on their way driving through town.

Lynville, Washington never ceased to make him feel

dismal. It was about eight thousand people or so. It was very traditional, very religious, and very humdrum with the biggest excitement being the town's fair, which of course Sam and his mom had not missed once since he was three. There were perfectly mowed lawns in front of well-kept houses, churches on almost every street corner, and a quaint historic downtown with antique shops and bakeries. It was like an even more wholesome version of The Stepford Wives if you even want to try to sleep with that idea.

Sam spent the better part of his time in the car watching the clouds and the trees and other mothers driving their sons to other doctor's appointments. Sam thought the sky was doing funny things. The sun was out and showing itself through the passing patches of dark clouds making it look like a big quilt, with bright blue sky behind the vivid gray clouds. Sam knew that the clouds above him were big puffy Cumulus clouds. He told his mother this and she asked where he learned such a big word.

"Book at school," was all he said. His attention was where he thought it should be and he did not feel the need for a very descriptive reply.

Cumulus clouds were potentially rain bearing but he hoped not. It was a very nice day out today and his hopes of taking advantage of the warm windy weather in his grandparents' backyard was something he was highly anticipating when they got back from the doctor's. Wilhelmina, his grandmother, would receive her Master Gardener's Degree from a university some years later. Her talent was no less now and the garden she tended to in her backyard resembled a small Eden. It was some sort of heaven-sent masterpiece of vivid vegetation, bright, beautiful flowers, shrubs, and a number of small trees, including a large vegetable garden with a large dirt box next to it. Sam would grab his small plastic bucket, a shovel and other random toys and go back behind the greenhouse which was a rosebush away, and play in the dirt box. His grandparents sometimes used this for compost and other excess clippings to play in. Sam loved playing in dirt and it was quite possibly his favorite thing to play with right next to sticks. Both were abundant, they were free, and they made excellent bombs and swords. There really wasn't anything else a…

Rambunctious ball of fail…?

…seven-year-old boy could possibly want except maybe some…friends? He kicked himself right as he said it. Nope, not gonna happen. They had arrived at the doctor's before he could play with his toys but this didn't bother him, he had been happily occupied otherwise.

Juliet locked the car and lead Sam into the large, pallid building downtown and they entered through the rotating doors. They crossed the marble flooring and went into the elevator pushing the button to be lead to the fourth level. The elevator door opened revealing a rather anticlimactic waiting area. The green carpet almost looked velvety and went well with the marble receptionist's desk and gold-colored elevator. Other than that, the white walls with pictures of lighthouses, plants and kittens were topped off with a terrible flowery trim that looked like it belonged in a rest home, making the entire room clash. It was like rest-home décor at its most nauseatingly finest. The receptionist told them that the wait would be about fifteen minutes and they took their seat in a couple of red chairs. Sam chose the chair next to the big fern plant to see if he could find any bugs on it, but the sham of a plant bore no such life.

About three feet from the receptionist desk, against the white wall, there was a stand with a tank of goldfish. Sam got up and walked over to see the fish a little closer. He peered up close until his nose was pressed right up to the glass; he watched how they swam around in the same circle. He thought they must be the luckiest fish in the world, enclosed in a wonderful, wet space, clear from any sort of predators, fed everyday, and in the company of other fish just like them. Sam wished he was a goldfish swimming around with other goldfish but he was not. He was all alone in the biggest fishbowl of them all: the world. And he wasn't sure how much longer he could keep on swimming before he lost all focus and drowned.

Not fifteen minutes after the goldfish had caught Sam's attention, a tall, older man in a suit with salt and pepper hair stepped out from the hallway and into the lobby. Sam did not know who he was but after seeing him shake his mother's hand he figured this must be the man that they had driven to see. Dr. Keuning walked over to Sam and introduced himself. Sam, still very nervous but, knowing he should be respectful, shook his hand back and introduced himself as well. They proceeded down the hallway until they reached a middle-sized office at the far end of the building's north face.

The room they entered was a typical office with a shelf of all types of books on different types of psychology including Lifespan, Child, Abnormal, and even a book on the psychology of sex, which of course Sam didn't know about yet and just found it to be a curious word. Close to the corner of the room, there was a cherry wood desk, and one of those leather chairs that let you spin around in it. It was surrounded by plaques indicating his many scholastic achievements and other accolades. He sat Sam and his mother down on the two chairs facing him, folded his legs exposing his wool socks, and began to ask questions. Sam tuned in and out of them depending if they were directed at him or not, he was looking over at the coloring station with childlike anticipation.

The doctor turned his attention to Sam for a few more minutes asking him certain questions and jotting down his responses on a yellow legal pad he had in his lap.

Doc: How old are you, Sam?

Sam: eight

Doc: What grade are you in?

Sam: second

Doc: Do you like your class?

Sam: no

Doc: Why not?

Sam: because I can't sit still and everyone hates me

Doc: Oh I'm sure everyone doesn't hate you.

How would you know? Teachers don't yell at you everyday, you don't have kids make fun of you behind your back. You get to sit in a big leather swivel chair and be smart for money, people like you. You're not an out of control eight-year-old with an irrepressible urge to be a hyperactive idiot you mean, stupid man. You're not me. People don't like me.

Sam: yes they do.

Doc: I'm sure they don't mean it.

Sam: then why do they say it?

The doctor answered with a question. Sam hated it when people answered with questions. It's like they were trying to avoid his question, like it wasn't good enough for them so they had to ask their own. He let it go.

Doc: Well Sam, if I gave you something that would help you concentrate and do better in school, would you like that?

Sam said that he guessed he would and the doctor scribbled a little more on his paper, talking to his mom and little more about whatever they were discussing. Sam, in the meantime, had been given permission by his mother to go and draw at the coloring table behind the doctor's couch. He sat there with the crayons and drew a picture of a black tornado in a giant, yellow wheat field approaching an old, red barn. Sam wished he could see a tornado. Being eight years old and still possessing a vivid imagination, he pictured himself flying through one, without getting a single scratch. Sam spent a lot of time in his head, more so than in the actual world. But the actual world was mean and nasty. Sam's world was nice and good and he liked it there.

"What do you say to that, Sam?" said his mother.

"What?" Sam confessed he hadn't been paying attention.

"The doctor thinks it's okay for you to go on some medication that's going to help with your ADHD, is that ok?"

"Yeah, that's fine," Sam said casually, reverting quickly back to his picture where he was making a group of people run in terror from the monster cyclone but the doctor quickly stole his attention away once more.

"Well Sam, I want to try you on a drug called Ritalin. It's this tiny white pill (he held up a sample of the drug in his fingers and it didn't look very impressive or seem to contain any brain altering substances but it was better than a horse tranquilizer) and you're going to take it three times a day and it's going to help you concentrate in school, ok?" Sam nodded his head in agreement.

"Ok then," said Dr. Keuning, "I've given you two weeks' worth of medication in there. I'm going to start you in at 40mg and see how you do with that. In two weeks when the medicine is gone I want you to come in and see me and tell me if there's been any changes or if you notice a difference in your behavior. Can you do that for me Sam?"

Sam said that he could and so the doctor scribbled the prescription on a piece of paper and gave it to his mother who put it in her purse. They both shook the doctor's hand and he escorted them to the secretary where Juliet quickly wrote a check and made another appointment. They went down the elevator, across the marble flooring, and out of the spinning doors to the car. On their way back home, Sam wasn't sure what he had just gotten himself into, but he hoped it was something that really *was* going to help him. Having this thought in his head he felt better already. He felt something he had not felt in long time: control. He smiled when he thought about it.

Christmas break went by as fast as ever and before he knew it, Sam Reed was back in that red building with the same familiar classmates as he had seen before he left. They all still looked the same and to no surprise of his they all still acted the same as well. Sam did not. Sam had a new surprise coming to everyone because he had something that nobody else in the school had—drugs.

Those sweet, beautiful pills of his and he was already feeling like someone who had just stepped out of a stuffy room into a cool summer breeze. He felt clear, he felt different, and he couldn't wait to show off this new, proud self to everyone he ran into. The bell signaled 7:45 and he joined the mass of children flooding into the big, metal doors and into their separate classrooms. Sam went into his and found his desk with no difficulty. Even though the teacher had arranged them differently than when they had left, Sam could see the sticker with his name on it for it was the only one that was doodled on and scratched up a bit while everyone else's was shiny and new looking. He put his lunch that his mom had made him that morning into his cubby and took his place.

Immediately the teacher started talking about the day's lesson and as usual Sam felt the urge to look at everything else around him to see if he could notice any changes but this time it was different. He could control the impulse and pay attention to what the teacher was saying. Sam wasn't shaking his legs or twiddling his thumbs as usual but engaged in the information that was being presented to him. He was focusing, he was sitting still, and he wasn't being a disruption.

Mrs. Clayton asked a question about what she had just

told everyone.

Sam raised his hand and answered it correctly; he smiled when the teacher smiled back at him. The sun peeked through the clouds and entered the classroom; it was going to be a good day for Sam Reed.

◆ ◆ ◆

February 1999

Ever since about the fourth grade, Sam's faith in God had steadily grown and matured and he believed that he was ready to take the next step in accepting God as his one and only savior. The church that Sam and his mother had been attending now for about eight years was having a tremendous influence on Sam. He enjoyed going and learning about everything that God and his word had to offer—so much so that one Sunday after service when the pastor had made an announcement that they were going to be offering a profession of faith class for anyone who was interested, Sam turned to his mother and told her that he wanted to take it.

"I'm glad you're enthusiastic, honey, but I think you might be too young, Sam. I'm not sure if you're ready to make that big of a commitment just yet, but maybe in a few years you can."

Although Sam was still rather young, he knew a challenge when he heard one and was not giving this up without a fight.

"Please mom! I really want to. I'll do anything it takes just please let me take that class!" Sam's voice was so convincing that his mother was left with little to even the score with and after several seconds of deep thought, turned to him and granted him permission to take the class.

"But you need to be diligent about this. You're dedicating yourself to God for the rest of your life and doing everything he expects you to do. You need to follow his rules and not disobey him."

"Mom, why would I want to disobey God? I love him…I really do."

"I know you do, but it won't be easy, you need to read your Bible and pray every day so you can be good, ok?"

Sam reassured her that he would be the best Christian that he could be and after finishing his conversation with his mother ran over to his pastor and told him of his decision to commit to being a Christian, which of course the pastor was delighted to hear! He told Sam that the first class started next week at four o' clock in the afternoon in room 112. Sam couldn't contain his excitement and he went home, not being able to stand the thought of waiting another week.

Four weeks later when he was all finished with his profession of faith class, the day had come for him, and two other girls that had taken the course with him, to go in front of the congregation and receive the plaque indicating that they had successfully finished the course. They would be ready to not only officially become followers of Jesus, but also be able to partake in communion, the breaking of the bread and the drinking of the cranberry juice which was symbolic of the blood of Christ. Before this commitment, Sam had always had to stay sitting down while his mother went up to participate with five hundred other adults to eat bread and drink some juice, definitely not easy for Sam. Although his intentions were pure and his thinking clear, at least this would give him an excuse to get up and move around a little bit before sitting back down. No matter though. Sitting or not sitting, he was headstrong on his commitment and eager to be able to truly call himself a Christian.

Prior to the ceremony at church, a party was held for Sam at Juliet's friends' house. Many members of the church as well as a couple of Sam's friends showed up with presents, cards, food, words of wisdom, and more. After everyone was full with cake and good spirit, they all circled around Sam in chairs and sofas. A few of the hundred kids sat on the floor. His mother was to his right, the pastor to the left.

"Now Sam," the pastor began, "I was asked to say a few words. I want to start off by telling you a story, a story that you're probably very familiar with and I'm going to emphasize something about it. It comes from the Bible: Mark, Chapter six, Verses 30-44." The pastor told the story of a time when Jesus and his disciples had been teaching all day and were tired and hungry, and boarded a small ship to go to a remote place to rest. Upon landing on the shore a small crowd was waiting for them and Jesus, having compassion on them began speaking the word of God to them. When he told his disciples to go to town to buy food they replied that eight months' wages would not be sufficient to buy enough food for all these people. When Jesus asked them what they had with them they replied five loaves of bread and two fish. Jesus took the bread, broke it and gave thanks. Then he asked his disciples to hand out the food to the people. When they had finished, twelve basketfuls of food remained and 5,000 people had eaten and were satisfied.

The pastor used this as a metaphor and explained to Sam that this was like the picture of his life.

"You see Sam, you may be little and not feel like a whole lot, but when you give yourself to God he can spread you around. He can turn you into something so much more than you think you are and he will use you to do great things. The step you've chosen to take tonight is the first one of many wonderful things that God has in store for you. Even though you may not feel like much, God can take what you are and multiply you by a thousand, allowing you to do so much more than you ever could have thought possible."

Sam thought of the idea of doing great things and liked the sound of it very much. That night, the ceremony at the church felt like an eternity but he was one of the centers of attention so this got him through it. The two other girls that had joined him in his profession of faith class were there too and the service revolved around them, but it really didn't. It was always about God, he came first in everything. The pastor retold his sermon of Jesus feeding the five thousand and then one of the girls performed a song. After a whirlwind of other activities, Sam along with the two others was asked to come up. Sam at 10 years old was dressed in black dress pants with a silk, brown-stripped, button up shirt, a clip on tie with a Taz from the Looney Tunes design all over it and black Reebok sneakers. Sam was an undisputed fashion icon in all his geek-ish glory.

Pastor Kaeman asked each one of them to stand where they were so they could be seen by the entire congregation and proceeded to ask each of them a series of questions in which they had to respond "I do." Sam was curious as to what would happen if he said 'No, I don't." He might be crucified, excommunicated, enslaved and tortured, or perhaps just asked to leave. He didn't want to upset the comfort zones. He obliged.

The first.

"Do you put your trust in Jesus as your savior, and as your Lord?"

Sam responded, "I do."

The second.

"Do you know that you belong to the family of God through your baptism?"

Sam once again responded, "I do."

The third.

"Do you commit yourself tonight that you continue to learn more and more about God and his word and that you will keep on serving him with your life and with your worship?" The question was of specific importance so it was asked to them all one more time, almost as if saying, *Are you sure you want to do this? You can say so now if you don't...speak up...No objections? Ok.*

"Am I sure?" he wondered to himself...*Beyond a shadow of a doubt, 100% positive that I will do this for the rest of my life?* The answer, at the time, was obvious and Sam responded for the last time.

"I do."

He now felt like he was married after all of the "I do's" and in a sense he was. He was married to God, to the faith, to the church, bound by holy matrimony to a belief that he would later forsake. If he had been told so that night, he would have laughed and walked off the other way. He knew no better. This was his life now and he thought that it would forever remain that way. He had made a permanent commitment to God and he was never going to break that promise, ever. Sam partook of communion and was very pleased with himself.

In his eyes, the life he had now would be the life he would always have. The thought of eventually growing up into a man and being able to venture out and experience what the world had to offer was a fairytale. Sam had not yet grasped that one day he was going to grow up and want to try grownup things. Most kids his age had the same mentality. Of course they thought of what they wanted to be when they grew up but actually being an adult was a far-fetched idea. Furthermore he was certain that the morals and principles, which he held onto now, would be with him for the better part of his life. He would never falter from God, he would never do anything the Bible said was wrong, and he would pursue the purpose that God had intended for him with the utmost passion and zeal. Sam did not factor in that evil has a plan for everyone as well, and the competition for his soul was a never-ending battle. Sam was still too innocent to know that real evil existed, because all he could see at the moment was the good. All he could see was the sun and the one who made it and knowing nothing else other than that, Sam proceeded with his innocent, spiritual, blissfully oblivious life as a ten-year-old.

Over the next four years, Sam had turned a complete 180-degrees from the second grade and had made a startling transformation. He was no longer the butt of ridicule anymore (just on occasion when no one else was left). He was becoming more and more able to control the majority of his impulses though he still had problems with some of the comments that he made to other people. This was understandable to most teachers and other adults though, as his mother had made clear to them that Sam's brain was still working out a few small kinks in the medicine. Socially, he had a lot of catching up to do but most importantly, now, he had friends; Real, genuine, honest to goodness, friends who he got to play with at recess. Some days were better than others though. Sam would sometimes be caught up in playing a game and to more dramatize blowing something up with his super powers he would throw rocks and dirt in the air which would hit someone in the head or get in a girl's hair. They would run and tattle on Sam who would end up getting into trouble. He had thankfully graduated from writing those lines on the white board and was usually sentenced to just hard time, which wasn't even so terrible; being as his teacher Mr. Trabenleim was still a very loving teacher and treated all of the kids in the classroom as if they were his own. He handled Sam especially well in the classroom and even had an assistant, Mrs. Chester, that would take Sam and a few other kids with the same problems into a separate room, dissect what the lesson had been about for them (this was usually for math, which was Sam's hardest subject) and would give them the special attention and help that they needed with certain assignments and projects. It helped out Sam tremendously and being as he had begun to see grades now instead of just "satisfactory" and "unsatisfactory" it was more important now that he do well in all of his subjects.

Earlier that week in a meeting with his mother, teacher, and the school counselor it had been explained to the both of them that Sam had a learning disability. When asked if he knew what this was, Sam guessed that it might be what kept him from being smart.

"No, no, Sam not at all," said the counselor. "In fact, if anything it makes you smarter. You just have a few disadvantages to overcome in order to use that intelligence."

"Like what?" Sam curiously inquired.

"Well some things might not make sense to you, but that's only because they're not being explained in a way that your brain can understand it."

His teacher, Mr. Trabenleim, spoke to Sam next.

"Sammy (he used affectionate nicknames for all of his students), do you remember what I was talking about last Thursday?"

Sam thought long and hard but was drawing a blank. He conceded defeat and finally sighed an embarrassed, "No."

The counselor then tried a different approach.

"Do you remember what it said on the board behind him?"

A light bulb flashed inside Sam and he went into brainpower mode listing that their had been lines on irregular verbs, the homework for the night, what the date had been, the fact that Mr. Trabenleim was wearing an athletic t-shirt with long blue jeans, and the conversation the two girls behind him were having. After he recalled all these things he just sat there like she had just asked him what time it was; as if it should be common knowledge to everyone in the room, but then realizing that he had just remembered all that his mouth sort of hung open for a few seconds.

"Now, Sam," said the counselor with a pleased smile on her face, "do you know how you remembered what you saw and not what you heard?"

Sam shook his head, befuddled.

"It's because you're what's called a 'visual learner.' You remember things by seeing them instead of hearing them. Other kids with learning disabilities are 'auditory learners' and they remember information better by hearing it rather than seeing it. You remembered all of those things because you saw them. You couldn't see what Mr. Trabenleim was saying so it only makes sense that you didn't retain the information. For instance, if someone wrote the word 'green' on the whiteboard in a red market and asked you what you saw you would say 'the color red.' Am I right?" Sam nodded. This was true. His brain was fine tuned to color and it was the first thing he always noticed about something, what color it was.

Sam tried to wrap his brain around itself. This was still all very confusing to him and he just wished he could be normal like all the other kids but knowing this was the way it was, just accepted it and prompted a question of his own. "Is there a medicine for it?" he asked

"I'm afraid not Sam, it's something that you have to work on yourself. You have to find a way of learning that works for you the best," which Sam thought was stupid but made sense. It was his brain, and he had to take responsibility for it.

"Mrs. Chester and I will keep helping you out in the classroom Sammy; it's nothing to be too worried about." Mr. Trabenleim sounded reassuring and Sam knew there really was nothing to fret over. Soon enough the meeting was over, as was the sixth grade. The easiest part of his life was officially over.

It had been only a year since Sam had made his profession of faith and he was still very immature in his walk with God. He had yet to encounter anything that would put this to the test. To say that Sam was not noticing girls would be untrue. It would be fair, however to say that he was not looking at them the way that other boys his age were. He never checked them out when they walked past him, he never looked down their shirts when they bent over and never told them to do that thing when boys they tell a girl to try and touch their elbows together so they can see their boobs get squished. Sam wasn't like that, he justified how he behaved by calling it respect. Any other guy his age would have called it "gay." Sam was so accustomed to being the odd one out, however, that he thought nothing of it. Sam had never heard the term "homo" before and wouldn't know what it meant even if he had. His sexual urges, though dormant for the time being, would gravitate towards men when they did come to term, and in fact when he started liking guys, he was not mature enough in his Christianity to know that it went against the faith. One day in art class when a girl caught a glimpse of Sam checking out her boyfriend, the idea that homosexuality was not encouraged in the seventh grade was about to hit close to home for Sam Reed.

Though Sam may have made some serious leaps in terms of development, he was still that awkward kid that nobody really wanted around. Though he wasn't necessarily the butt of ridicule, he was still an easy target and as Sam would soon find out—nothing was sacred. Now entering the seventh grade and quite possibly one of the most difficult times in his life, he knew this, but didn't care. He had accepted that he was an unwanted person and that being popular and well liked was something that he was not. Cliques and groups had been established years before and Sam had not found one to belong to. He was destined to forever be on the island of misfit toys and as important as it was to still somehow manage his way into the preps and jocks, knew his place and stayed there, uncomfortably. For sometime now, ever since the beginning of the year, he had been very interested in women, but not in a sexual sense like the rest of the boys his age who were now going into the chrysalis of puberty. He wanted to be friends with girls, so he could have people to connect with being the energetic, flamboyant, and most of all rather feminine individual that he was blossoming into. However, this was not to say that Sam wanted to just come and say that he was a homosexual. This would be a terribly unwise thing to do in the seventh grade and he wanted to date a pretty girl, mainly to make everyone else believe that he was just like them. Speaking of pretty girls, there was this certain little gal that was in Sam's grade that he had taken a particular fancy to. She was new to the school that year and her name was, and still is Tana. Captivated by the beauty of the girl that shared the same space he did, he was almost certain that the case of his being gay was quite the opposite even though there was no escaping it. He got out of class one day and casually followed her to her locker, hoping he would get a decent chance to ask her out.

Before he could reach her, three of her friends intercepted him. Their faces were smeared with expressions of disgust. The middle girl, Brittany spoke first. She was the type of girl with parted blonde hair with short shorts and a somewhat low cut t-shirt, as low as she could go without getting asked by the school to go home and change. She was the ringleader, and the other two were her lionesses, hungry for meat.

"We heard that you were planning on asking Tana out Sam…is that true?" there was a bitter look on her face as if even talking to him even if she was about to publicly disgrace him caused her grief and shame like she would have to take a shower afterwards.

Sam was going to completely deny this but decided on just coming out with it. If they were here to torment him about it they may as well get their comments in now instead of afterwards.

"Yeah, it's true, why?" Sam spoke with a shyness that he couldn't help and all three girls, wanting Sam to have no confidence in the situation whatsoever, picked up on it immediately and took full advantage of it.

"Well she's not interested in you."

"Oh, did she say that?"

"No, she didn't, does she have to?" the girl on the left, a brunette, said this.

"Well, I don't think you can say that she's not interested if you haven't even asked her yourself."

"We don't need to ask, Sam. Don't you know that awesome girls like Tana don't date faggots like you?"

All three of them laughed at this, Sam just scowled at them, in an embarrassed manner, and then came back with "I'm not a faggot, don't call me that!"

"Why are you trying to hide it from everyone? It's not like we all haven't figured it out by now." This was not said in a comforting tone and Sam was getting very uncomfortable.

"How can I be gay? I'm asking a girl out, right? So I can't be one."

"Well we think you are, and so does everyone else. It's obvious that the only reason you would ask a girl out is to establish a cover to make everyone think you like girls when you really don't. Tana is just gonna be a part of your little cover game. Well, we're her friends and that's a really shitty thing to do, so we're here to stop you."

"Shut up," said Sam, in a sort of "whatever" kind of tone. "If she wants to reject me, then she can do it herself. And for your information I'm asking her because I like her."

"Aw, you're so trying to cover yourself it's pathetic. We see the way you look at guys and we're not the only ones. And do you really think she's going to go for you? I mean, you're like, a *nobody* and she's popular and actually good-looking."

Sam couldn't escape that one; he was being cornered and he was starting to panic. This couldn't go beyond the parameters of this conversation.

"Just leave it alone," Sam said, getting more and more irritated. "I'm not gay. I've never even kissed anyone so how could I possibly know what I like."

"Don't deny it, Sam," said Brittany. "It's only going to be more embarrassing when everybody finds out that you like boys."

The thing you need to know about Sam Reed is that at this point in his life he was currently on two different medications, one for his ADHD and one anti-depressant, which combined were doing minor damage to his brain and slightly worsening his brain to mouth control. Whatever Sam had in his head had no safeguard from getting out no matter how much trouble it may have gotten him in. This condition was made worse when he was in situations of high emotional stress or great excitement. Sam was certainly in a highly stressful situation and not able to filter what was coming out. Not only was he beginning to feel threatened, the lions were cornering him, licking their hungry teeth with their tongues and in his attempt to actually defend himself for the first time, he played the absolute last, and worst card that he had in his possession and he played it with authority.

"Well nobody's gonna find out about it if you three bitches keep your mouths shut!"

Big mistake.

In fact, Sam Reed had just made one of the biggest mistakes of his life. He had not only simultaneously just swore, something he had never done before, let alone to girls, which could get him in big trouble with just about anybody, he had also tried to step up and out of his precinct of where he stood in the scholastic social ladder. The outcast had just insulted the preps. He had disrupted the comfort zones of the superior and for that he was about to pay with every ounce of dignity he had. There was no doubt that he was about to get it. Tears were welling up and he knew he was about to cry, but he was getting so angry that instead of just storming off with a tear-stained face, he kept on going, he wanted to fight the power, and he wanted to win.

"*What* did you just call us?" said one girl with a look that showed Sam that she had absolutely heard what he had called them and intended to do something about it.

Sam retaliated once more. "Well, you called me a faggot. That's not very cool either."

"That's because you *are* a faggot, faggot!"

This was not what Sam was anticipating and with his emotions rising, he lashed back without even thinking about what he was about to say, tributaries of angst flowing rabidly through his hot bloodstream, "Then if I'm a faggot, you're a bitch!"

Bigger mistake. Sam's ammunition was running low, but so was Brittany's patience and what he had just said did not amuse her and her band of sluttish sorority sisters in the least, and the look on Brittany's face changed from cold hearted, to cold-blooded revenge. Sam almost knew what he had coming to him.

"Hey everybody!" She spoke so that every head in the

hallway turned to their direction with anticipation. Then she spoke the words that would echo through his head for the rest of his middle and high school life and she spoke them proudly, and callously. Words so simple, it almost seemed as if they could do no damage, while in fact he knew what was coming and thought that maybe people would just ignore her, but they wouldn't. Those words were about to turn Sam's comfortable world into a living hell and looking him straight in the eyes as she said it made the sting that much more excruciating.

"Everybody…Sam Reed is a faggot!"

Dead silence except for the echo of her statement…a perfect slow motion echo. It was almost beautiful how it reverberated down the corridors of the school. It hit every metal bit of every locker, went through every ear, and returned back again. But the silence was short-lived.

Then the laughter started, slow at first and then it began to grow louder and more vicious. Students up and down the hallway were pointing and laughing at Sam, and he thought this might just be a bad dream but when he shut his eyes and re-opened them, it was still happening. Sam just stood there absolutely mortified, frozen with every single eye that was in the hallway directly on his with expressions ranging from humor to shock. Clearly, everyone was not going to side with him. Names were being hurled at him like lightning bolts.

"Fuckin' homo!" shouted the boy across from them. The laughter continued, it continued from all directions, he couldn't escape; there was nowhere else to run.

"Sam's gay!" someone had coughed while walking by.

Other similar comments were being shouted out by kids all around him, but what hurt the most was seeing the kids that he looked up to laughing at him, mocking him, killing him without even knowing they had knives. He looked back at the girl who had started this with a look that questioned how she could do something like this but he knew how. She was just a bleeding bitch who would have done this even if he wasn't planning on asking any girl out. Tana for all he knew might have been just a red herring. Their mission was clear and now it was complete. Sam Reed was being humiliated in front of the entire school.

He didn't know what to do, everyone was laughing, and everyone was pointing. He was exposed, naked, and so vulnerable. He did the only thing he knew how to do at that point; he ran in the opposite direction, just flat out ran from everything. He ran until he was out the metal doors of his school and then he kept running, he was trying to escape the laughter but as he ran it only echoed harder and more vindictive. He ran and kept running until he no longer had the energy to continue with it. He started to walk, and then he started to rain, knowing life was about to get no better from here on out. He noticed black clouds in the sky were approaching and he wanted to be taken by them, by the blackness. He looked back at the building that would surely be the death of him in the weeks to come. It was now clear to him that he was not welcome anywhere near there again, or anywhere else either. He noticed nothing else around him, but just began going into hysteria, crying, almost screaming as he made his frantic way into the approaching storm; into the darkness.

Part II:
Darkness & The Hound of the Basket Case

Darkness: (adj) characterized by gloom. Dismal; lacking or having very little light. Sullen or threatening.

The thing under my bed waiting to grab my ankle isn't real,
I know that, and I also know that if I'm careful to keep my foot under
the covers, it will never be able to grab my ankle.
    -Stephen King

Once riding in old Baltimore, heart filled head filled with glee,
I saw a Baltimorean keep looking straight at me.
Now I was eight and very small, and he was no whit bigger
And so I smiled, but he poked out his tongue and called me "Nigger."
I saw the whole of Baltimore from May until December;
Of all the things that happened there, that's all that I remember.

   -Countee Cullen, *"Incident"*

The mind is its own place, and in itself,
can make a heaven of hell or a hell of heaven.

   -John Milton

Like one who, on a lonely road, doth walk in fear and dread
And having looked back once, walks on, and turns no more his head
Because he knows a frightful fiend doth cloth behind him tread.

   -Samuel T. Coleridge, *"The Rime of the Ancient Mariner"*

April 2001

The looming storm clouds above provided Sam no comfort as he walked home. In the distance, the crackle of thunder could be vaguely heard and although it was not raining, there was a stagnant and ominous silence in the atmosphere that made him feel as though all weather-hell may break loose at any point. He had stopped the worst of the crying a while ago but the wound he felt inside was still felt very fresh. He knew full well that this was a burden that he carried on his own. He allowed what was going on with the other kids to continue happening without really telling anyone about it, or at least without telling anyone who could do anything about it, but therein lay his dilemma. If he ran to an adult or a supervisor he would be seen as more of a wuss than he already was and the humiliation and mockery would continue, maybe even get worse. On the other hand, if he actually grew a pair and stood up for himself for a change he might actually…he might actually get punched in the face more.

Doubt settled inside of him and made itself at home.

Looking at it from a logical standpoint, running away certainly might work but it wasn't like it was something he could make last forever. He would eventually have to face his "classmates" head on and when that happened, well, he imagined it would be like wandering into a lion's den wearing a suit made out of gazelle meat; he would undeniably be eaten alive without any hesitation from them. It didn't take a rocket scientist to figure out that Sam had no physical strength whatsoever and would most likely lose any sort of fistfight. His sense of sarcastic wit had yet to even be conceived, in fact as far as he was concerned he hadn't even shot the load yet. Sam had never fought a soul, never dissed anyone, and had never sworn once in his life until recently. He was about as innocent as innocent came and he supposed this might be one of those times where having a father might have actually come in handy, but the reality was, he would have to get himself out of this jam sooner or later and he was going to have to do that on his own. That was the only way he saw fit to take care of all of this.

When he got home he noticed a note on the table that read, "Pills on the counter, I'll be home at seven for dinner. Love, Mom."

There were multiple trips to see Dr. Keuning, and one recently regarding some new medication that he had suggested putting Sam on. There had been no reason to take him off of the Ritalin that he was already on and he had never exhibited any sort of side effect from it either, but Dr. Keuning had suggested they "experiment" with some different medications to see if they might work better. The doctor had told them to come back and see him in a week or two if any negative side effects started evolving from it. Assured that there should be nothing aside from appetite loss and mild depression (which he had given him another pill for) they took the wise doctor up on his advice and got the meds.

Sam examined the tiny capsules all locked away inside of the clear orange cylindrical cage. He twisted off the childproof cap and popped one in his mouth.

"Cheers, Doc."

He vacantly made his way up the stairs and into his bedroom and lay there, everything still fresh like paint in his mind: the laughter, the pointing, the humiliation, oh the fucking humiliation. That would never dry, that would always be fresh and discouraging.

Right away, like he had been programmed to do this, he pulled out his notebook and a scrawny yellow, slightly chewed, Ticonderoga pencil, both from the same backpack and began to write. He didn't know why he was writing, but for some odd reason he felt that was the best way to get everything out and so this is what he did. After his fit of writing therapy, he looked down at what he had.

Something's no fun
Something's undone
Someone's on the run
I don't appreciate those misinformed rumors.
Just, stop ok?
Please stop laughing at me.
Concealed by a cloak
Life is a joke
Leads me to choke
There's no cause for those cutting stares
I mean it.
Please stop laughing at me.
Save all your shivers

Pull out your slivers
Cry me a river
There's no reason for that kind of language.
Really, I'm quite serious.
Please stop laughing at me.
I'll never hear cheers
For embracing my tears
I'm chased by my fears
Physical violence isn't necessary,
I'm asking you for the last time
Please stop laughing at me.
I can't find a haven
To be saved from the raven
It's my bones he's a cravin'
Blood has been spilled
A hole's still unfilled
My body is chilled
Will somebody kindly fetch a mop?
There's a tiny pool of blood in the boy's bathroom
I told you to stop.
You wouldn't.
I had to.
Please stop laughing at me.

"What a joke," he thought to himself, but not being someone to throw away anything he wrote, Sam just stuffed the paper into the drawer in the nightstand by his bed and went back to being a nobody.

"Where are you God?" he wondered out loud needing some Christ-like consolation right about now.

God didn't answer. He hadn't answered him in prayer

lately and it made Sam feel disconnected from the one entity he was taught was always there. Maybe God was making fun of him, too.

That night before he went to sleep he got down on his knees and prayed for that same old Jesus to help him be a stronger person emotionally. For now that was the best that he could do, sticking it out for as long as he could without cracking under pressure. It didn't sound too hard. All he had to do was ignore everyone around him, just shut 'em right out and keep walking with his head low, legs moving swiftly, and his face covered as much as possible and pretend there was nothing wrong even though the truth was that there were all sorts of wrong with this kid. The bowling of thunder was nearer and the bullwhips of lightning lit up the dark night sky. The storm outside was here, and so was the one inside Sam Reed. Tears had already begun their descent from eye to cheek, from chin to sheet.

He fell asleep as soon as it started to rain.

Then he began to dream a little dream.

He awoke with a start. It was still nighttime, but he was not in his bed. He was out on a street in another part of town. The streetlamps flickered on and off momentarily, casting bits of light on the cold, damp pavement that he was walking on; normally at first and then cautiously, as if he were anticipating something jumping out to get him. When no such fiend showed itself, Sam returned to his normal stride and continued walking down the road not knowing what was going to happen next. Houses from Lynville both familiar and unfamiliar were strewn across from the sidewalks with exaggerated features. Sam who was of course dreaming thought nothing of these, or of the fact that even though it was nighttime there were yellow storm clouds above him and a calm wind running through the trees of a nearby forest. It seemed like it was daytime, but it was night; it had to be. Shadows and objects seemed to move and watch him as he carefully walked along the road expecting everything and overlooking nothing as if he were somehow lost somewhere in The Twilight Zone. That was probably what was going on. He was there, and Rod Sterling was going to walk out from behind a building in a polished suit to introduce Sam and his predicament to the audience any second.

"There is a fifth dimension beyond that which is known to man. It is a dimension as vast as space and as timeless as infinity. It is the middle ground between light and shadow, between science and superstition, between the pit of man's fears and the summit of his knowledge. It is the dimension of the imagination. Sam Reed has found himself in this dimension: a polymerization of midnight and sunrise, of life and of death. Through this he will die in order to live, and live in order to die. Sam Reed had found himself as an abscess on his own mind. He will have to detach himself from his own imagination or perish forever in the perverse wastelands here…in The Twilight Zone."

"Thanks Rod, you always know how to make a sweatin' bullets kind of situation look even more unimaginably bleak don't you, you slick-haired little rat!"

A cool mist was off in the near distance skulking, creeping along the grass and onto the road seeming to eat everything it came into contact with. It looked to be only silver vapor but upon closer inspection, Sam noticed a small gray dot of some kind in the middle of the fog. It did not move with the fog or with the wind but stayed where it was, remaining motionless and beginning to grow larger with every step Sam took in its direction. Not being able to contain his curiosity, he began to move closer to the mysterious darkness, but as he did, a horrid noise rose from the mist. It started in low and then it began to escalate into a louder, more distinct sound. He recognized it soon enough as the growling of a dog. A definite "Bark" and the heavy sound of metal chains were uncomfortably present. There was a dripping sound, like a running faucet, but it sounded much thicker than water. As Sam was now only meters away he saw very clearly just what kind of dog it was.

The bestial creature stood about four feet high on all fours with hair as black and odious as the shadow from which it had emerged; it was not scraggly or unkempt but sleek and smooth with a beautiful black luster to it. The paws it walked with were as normal as any hound's, but its claws were that of a grizzly bear's with red stains on all of them; blood. It opened its jaws to reveal rows of teeth almost resembling small knives protruding inside its mouth. But the feature that stood out most of all was the dog's eyes. They were striking balls of cobalt blue, and they were human eyes. The eyes looked at Sam with an unholy intention. The dog came closer and to some surprise on Sam's part, began to speak. When it spoke, it was like no human Sam had ever heard speak and though the voice itself seemed to be a person's, it was not. There was a demeanor in the voice that was positively grisly, a blood curdling voice so cold and so satanic; it froze Sam to the spot.

"So here I find you. I've been waiting for you, Sam. Oh yes I have, waiting for so long until the moment when I can find you here all alone in your head. You don't know how badly I want you Sam. I want to taste you, eat you, to devour you, and I want your body to be inside of mine. I'll start by eating your fear as a snack and once you've been drained of that I'll lunge toward you with my teeth and begin to tear you to shreds starting with your chest, then I'll slash open your neck and sink my hungry fangs into your face breaking your skull in one easy bone-shattering crunch. And when you're lying dead on the pavement, blood running into the gutters, I'll drag you back to hell in my cold, stained jaws and there you'll be all better Sam. You'll be brand new with not a scratch on you so that way every time I kill you, every time you scream for me to stop and you writhe and twist painfully on the ground it will be a fresh kill. I shall lick your bones every time I am finished and then you'll be back again and I can keep killing you Sam and continue to slit your throat and lick my paws and there's

going to be nothing you can do about it because you'll be in my basement, my home, my heaven will be your hell Sam and what a hell it shall be. There's only one way out of this, Sam and you know what that way is. You have to kill yourself. Kill yourself before I do it for you and then you might be spared the greatest horror you have ever known. This is a warning Sam and if I ever have to see you in your dreams again I can't promise that I'll be so forgiving. Kill yourself; do away with your sickening innocence once and for all."

And with a last gnash of teeth the beast was gone, lost in the shadows, lost in hell. The environment around him changed and he noticed a pain shooting through him like a full body Charlie horse; it dropped him to his knees and curled him up like a fetus. There was blood all over him that flowed freely out of every crevasse of his body; ears, eyes, nose, mouth, everywhere was dripping with the crimson substance and with one last attempt at salvation Sam screamed but before the sound was halfway out of his body, it was over just like that, and he found himself back in his bed.

It was three o' clock in the morning.

There was no mist, no blood, and no hound; just his sweaty, scared-shitless self. The words the devil dog had hissed at him continued to echo perfectly through his ears. He looked down and found his sheets had been soiled with a considerable amount of piss but he didn't care, he was too scared to care.

After regaining some sort of composure, he went to the bathroom to grab new sheets to dress his bed with and then Sam returned to the confines of his room, shut the door, and held on to his teddy bear in his shaking arms as tight as he could, his tear-filled eyes wide and red, with his broken mind fixed on the thought that he was beginning to go insane. Sam Reed knew that either one of two things was happening: the pills he took earlier had either terrible, mind-altering side effects or he had been challenged by the devil.

Perhaps even a sadistic combination of the two. Whatever it was, he slept no more that night.

The next morning he told his mother that the pills he had taken yesterday had given him a terrible nightmare and she said to just keep taking them as to not upset his brain even more. She would make an appointment with the doctor and they would go in to see him as soon as she could find some time off from the bank. Sam looked at the devilish pill sitting on the table. Bare and full of mind poison, he reluctantly swallowed it with a splash of orange juice, ate about half of his egg and said he would eat the rest of it later. He had said he just wasn't hungry at the moment. Part of him was frozen on the dream last night.

"...there's only one way out of this, Sam."

One way out of what? There was no way out of middle school, it was required. Juliet would have had him home schooled if she'd had the time but she had to work so much as it was. Sam would just have to live with it for now.

"Kill yourself before I do it for you."

In the days and weeks that followed the incident at school, the twelve-year-old boy was left lost in distress and the vivid dream a few nights ago had allowed his thoughts to fare no better. Sam continued to keep to himself like the evolving anomaly he was; separating himself from crowds was a trade that he was rapidly perfecting. School was a fading memory, the people in it just blurs racing by him. He had his own cloud looming over him. He had been absolutely terrified; for a nightmare of this magnitude had never entered his mind before and he was so shocked of having it that the thought of killing himself was a very real possibility. Either that or he would certainly go without sleep for a considerable amount of time. Sooner or later however, he would have to close his eyes. When he did he would dream, and the hound would return again giving him no way out. For three days and three nights he thought of it, of doing it. He contemplated how he might make it happen that afternoon after school while he stood over the bathtub inside his home, water dripping from the faucet, exposed and defenseless in his unstable being. The desire and the fantasy seemed to coil together into one surreal and lurid state. He saw a shimmer of light from the reflection of the water and imagined the shine of a razor, and then felt himself holding the smooth, sharp object in his hands. He imagined the three-inch-long piece of metal and he saw it glaring at him, he knew it was taunting him, egging him on from within the barriers of his fragile, compromised mind. He shut his eyes hard.

Time to pretend,

Pretend me dead,

Dead in my head,

Instead of being fed good thoughts in my bed, I'm led by my head to pretend that I'm dead.

Sam saw the vision as if his eyes had never shut. He imagined himself standing across from the room witnessing it happening right in front of him. It was horrifying, yet so beautiful and so vivid. He saw himself naked, but it was more than just naked without clothes; it was the vulnerable kind of naked too, as if he were standing in a crowded courtroom in front of a gaunt, towering judge and being sentenced for a crime he had no control over committing. The entirety of the room held their yellow judgmental eyes on him and he could hear their whispers about him seep into his ears. The hound was sitting in the back, as wicked and as pleased as ever. He imagined the judge atop his perch grabbing his desk and leaning in close to his face, surveying him with a gross fetidity.

"Samuel Brandon Reed this court finds you guilty on all charges. We care not to hear of your rebuttals, pleas, or inconsequential arguments. You must be sentenced to immediate and severe death for disrupting the comfort zones of the superior. You knew the rules, you did, and we know you did! Thought you could pretend those rules didn't apply to you, eh? Thought you could play the naïve victim but that isn't how any of the others play the game. You were told to be quiet, you were told to be invisible and you just couldn't do that much, could you? Could you? No, we tried to do away with the likes of you plenty of times already but enough is just never enough for you, is it? Of course it isn't. Well there's not much else to be said here. Go to your bath and draw your water, slip into those inviting waters and let the blood trickle out of you slowly, so slowly that when it comes out of your veins and into the water it's like a foreigner in a new country and it hesitates before descending to the bottom of the tub to plume outward. And right before you die, right before that last glimmer of life escapes you and you lie dead in that red, glossy water, we'll come in to see you; we want to see you Sam, we want to see that before you left this world that you learned your lesson. To never disturb what ought not be disturbed ever again. NOW AWAY WITH YOU!!"

The judge slammed down his gavel, which snapped the boy out of the daydream. The tub was a little over half full with hot water. The steam was rising all around, hazing the room with a thick layer of clear vapor. He grabbed a chair from the downstairs kitchen and placed it right next to the tub, took the halogen lamp from beside his bed and placed it on the chair, turning it on and letting it dance upon the water. It reflected like fragments of glass in the sun. He just stared at it, like those eyes in the courtroom stared at him...like the hound had stared at him, except, he was still not able to attack. The hound was the only one who could attack. He had to sit, wait, and be patient, and be the victim, not the killer. He was never meant to be the killer, just the one who was killed.

He was waiting for the water to leap out of the tub and sprout imaginary hands, grab him, and tug him into its bowl and swallow him whole. He looked at the blade that was in his hand and felt so much inside of him, yet a great deal of nothing at the same time. Sam was injected with fear and paralyzed with the uncertainty of what his next move would be, as if his body was conscious but his mind was in some sort of dream- induced coma and this was all part of the haze inside that dream. *The haze, oh the haze, the wonderful haze, that wondrous and grand miasma of concealed mystery. How he wished he knew it better so he could pilot his way out of the haze, that dismal fog of perpetual limbo.*

He thought perhaps that if he lost himself enough, hid in one of his mind's corners that maybe he could stay there and no one or no thought would find him and eventually all of this would go away and everything would be alright. Wouldn't that be just terrific? Just fine and dandy, just as swell as swell could be.

His mind created the hell and he imagined it, once again, like it was real. He saw himself posing in the tub, one leg over the side and one in the water. One hand was placed, palm down next to the side of the tub and the blood trickled down from it, the other hand was in the tub filling the water with the red, sticky substance while the light was still dancing about, creating a glitter effect. Then he imagined the police who were there investigating the death. He saw them standing there befuddled, unsure of what to scribble down on their pads of paper, muttering to one another in amazement and saying to each other:

"See that Samuel Reed there in that tub, he may be dead now but son-of-a-gun, he put on one hell of a performance, didn't he? That kid went out with a bang, he did."

It would all be grand indeed, but he was doing it again, he was lying to himself. He knew deep within his heart of hearts that life, yes, was escapable but the pain was not. It would linger even after the last drop of blood hit that bathtub floor. He remembered reading an excerpt from

Dante's Inferno in his English class. How the spoilers and suicides ended up in the second round of the seventh circle of hell known as the Woods of Suicides. Where they were imprisoned inside of thorn trees and harpies would make their homes in them, tearing off their branches and causing them terrible, inescapable anguish while blood dripped from their branches. The spoilers would be chased through the forest by starving, snapping dogs not being able to rest. He wondered for a moment if this in fact was the job of the hound he had met but decided not to dwell on it. He knew overall this was not at all a fate he wanted. As much as he sought to escape the pain, and he almost once put that blade up to his wrists for his "goodbye cruel world" moment, he knew better, and did not. Sam went downstairs and placed the knife back on the kitchen counter and slipped into the tub without it. He bathed without any rash theatrics and just contemplated it all, questions fired like gunshots in his brain. What would he do come tomorrow? He knew the hound would be back and knowing that he was not ready to face it, refused to close his eyes, but he was going on his third day without sleep and the bath was soothing him so he got out and went to his bed. He tried not to close his eyes but he was losing his fight to stay awake with every ticking second. It was nine pm and very dark outside. There was no rain, just the hums of the night. He briefly closed his eyes and hoped tomorrow might not be as bad as he thought it might be.

He fell asleep within minutes.

The usual sound of birds and the familiar smell of breakfast heralded the morning and, Sam got out of bed. The sun was just barely creeping over the mountains, beginning the day in the small, semi-bustling world that was

Lynville. He was so close to smiling when all of a sudden the events of the other day hit him like a lightning bolt of depression and he remembered that today was not going to be a good day. The rest of the morning leading up to school was sort of conglomerated into one fuzzy event. Wakeupgetdressedgodownstairseatbreakfastbrushteethtake medskissmomwalkoutdoor. That's what it felt like. That's what it was. Before he could even compose himself he was already there. Right outside those monstrously intimidating metal doors that were his middle school. He breathed at least a hundred deep breaths before finally composing himself and thinking of what route he could take that would attract himself the least amount of attention. Sooner or later he would have to go to class and face everybody. He figured that instead of ducking and trying to avoid everyone he might as well get all the harassment over with and opened the doors. Luckily Sam had gotten there rather early so there really wasn't a whole bunch of people there yet and there were no eyes on him yet so he just bolted for his class, not frantically, just a little faster than usual. He opened the door to find no one else there and was relieved by this. He sat down in the back and opened up a book, burying himself in it. It was not long until 7:35 came by and the first bunch of kids, a group of girls, came walking through the door. Sam was waiting for the snide remarks to come flooding out and he heard them all in his mind but none came. He had to admit he was slightly offended but very relieved when the girls sat down a few rows over from him and continued talking as if he were not there. But he wasn't there, not to them at least, and he knew this. In this situation, it was better to be ignored than noticed and he went back to his book. A few minutes later, more kids came flooding in and sat down, none by Sam though. This distance was welcomed but curious, they all began talking in their groups and a subdued laughter was distilling throughout the room. Sam briefly looked up from his book and noticed a few eyes were on him. He knew they were talking about him, he just knew.

Sam spent lunchtime with the school's counselor. He would do this for the rest of his middle school years, talking about why he wasn't popular and reasons he didn't fit in and ways that he would be able to work on it. To no avail did any of the methods ever work. He tried to be as friendly as he possibly could without having an aneurysm but kids just proved one thing: middle school was that pivotal moment in life where everybody found out who wasn't good enough to be friends with anyone else and this psychology was shared until they graduated high school. Sam just happened to be one of those people. It was all such a blur anyway that he could barely remember anything good about middle school despite his best efforts. All he remembered was being outed, being laughed at, and being in the way of everyone else who was trying to live their lives without him. Sometimes he wished he really was dead but he knew better than that. He would never want it to be by his own hand, he just wished he would curl up and die, as peacefully as it could happen.

It was the summer before Sam took that uncomfortable leap into high school. He and his mom were on their way to a mountain camping lodge, northeast of Lynville, called Silver Lake. The drive up was a good hour or so of winding roadways, stop signs, and camouflaged towns. The drive up the mountain was always enjoyable for the both of them, and by Sam in particular. The vastness and color was breathtaking and he absorbed as much of it in as he could. From his house, nothing up here seemed to exist, like it had all just been painted on the world's largest canvas; with streaks of lavender that fixed themselves on the speckled granite slopes and brushstrokes of pine and emerald which made up the towering firs and pines that kept watch over the surrounding wilderness.

They had been there about a week already with their familiar regiment of paddle-boating and rock collecting coming to a close. They were having one last dinner of hot dogs and brown beans around the campfire, not saying much but just enjoying each other's company and their meal.

"Are you excited to start high school?"

"Eh, yes and no. I feel like it might be middle school with more older and more educated idiots."

Juliet smiled.

"You'll be just fine, just try your best to focus on school. We're going to have you on that new medicine so that should help."

More drugs, he thought. "Yippee for me," he rubbed his stomach back in forth.

"I don't feel so hot mom, think I'm going to call it an early night."

"Ok, do you need anything?"

"Nah, I should be ok, I just need to lie down."

They exchanged goodnights and Sam went to bed.

He woke up what seemed like seconds later feeling much worse. It was already 10:37 in the morning.

A jolt of sickness slithered through his body and he fell out of the cot in the tent moaning out in pain and waking his mother up.

"Sammy what's wrong!?"

"I don't know."

He threw up, everywhere. All over the place. Remnant of last night's course could be seen floating about in the gross substance.

"Oh, goodness," Juliet mumbled, slightly panicking.

He threw up again.

She panicked more this time, and before she could let herself register that this was a serious situation, Sam began to convulse.

Juliet threw the entire tent (vomit and all) and the rest of their belongings into the trunk of the car while Sam who had found temporary refuge on a log continued to vomit. Juliet finished fast, picked Sam up and placed him the backseat.

"We're going to the doctor, Sam. Just hold on and we'll be there as soon as we can." Her frightened tone was not reassuring but Sam nodded his head anyway. He felt like every muscle in his body, every organ and blood vessel was writhing and intertwining together, for no reason but to cause him more pain and distress. He threw up again.

The doctor's office was about an hour away from where they had been camping and the speed limit was a constant 45 almost the entire way there.

Juliet wasn't thinking about any sort of speed limit. The trees and mountains that had been so beautiful coming up were now blurs as though the portrait on which they had been freshly painted on before had been smeared and it all just smudged together.

Sam rolled down the window to throw up more.

"Hang on Sam, Oh dear God, please."

He passed out and came to when his door clicked open.

Sam tried to stand but found he couldn't even walk and Juliet, who at this point was fueled by parental adrenaline, carried him inside the doctor's office. They took him in right away and after examining him the doctor confirmed that Sam was in a state of dehydration and needed to be taken to the hospital immediately. The doctor called ahead so they would be expected. Juliet drove like a bat out of hell to the hospital, about 35 minutes away. After she parked the car, she carried him across the parking lot and in through the emergency room doors. They got him into a wheelchair.

He threw up again. It was coming up like clockwork, every five to ten minutes a fresh batch of puke was making its way up and out.

The receptionist directed them to the elevator and told them to go to the fourth floor nurses' station. Sam felt as though he was almost paralyzed as his mother wheeled him into the elevator telling him to try and keep his eyes open and that everything...

"...There, there Sammy, Mom's here...shhh shhhh don't worry...everything will be alright."

"Everything?"

"Everything...

...will be alright."

The words still had the same effect on her as they had so many years ago. It was looking into her son's innocent eyes that triggered this inside of her. The comfort and the unease. She knew she had to say it to make him feel better, but what if it wouldn't? What if it all went downhill from here? What if he didn't make it? What if...

"Mom?"

She looked down at him.

"Am I going to be okay?" was all he would say for the next day or so before he passed out, but he asked with a curious power in his tone as if he wanted to know this and only this before he went into the blackness.

Juliet smiled, she would always smile in these kinds of situations because she knew she had to. Sam was her boy, her young man, and her blessing. If anything ever happened to him...well, she wouldn't let her mind go there.

"Everything will be alright, Sam." Juliet began to hope for the mantra's truth to be realized.

He closed his eyes and everything was dark.

The elevator opened and Juliet rushed Sam to the nurse's station. It was the afternoon but it was not terribly busy so a crowd of nurses huddled around the mother and her child.

"Ma'am you need to bring him this way, we have a room ready for him."

Juliet wheeled Sam into the room the nurse directed her to and immediately placed him carefully on the bed. The nurses escorted Juliet out of the room, insisting that they needed to watch over him now and give him immediate medical attention. They quickly hooked Sam up to the intravenous tube, reviving him with streams of hydrating fluid. They worked with care and explained everything to his mother as they went through the procedure. Julie sat there, exhausted, but relieved that her son was in the best place and getting the best care possible.

An hour and a half went by but it felt like days.

"You again, eh?"

"What?" said Sam, cocking his head slightly.

"It's you, you've come back I see."

"Who are you?"

"An old codger, unlike you, so young and free."

"I'm Sam." he introduced himself, not really knowing what else to do.

"I know who you are."

"How do you know me, can you read my mind?"

"Known you my whole life, son."

"Am I dead?"

"Dunno, I haven't decided that yet. Would you like to be? I have a room ready for ya if you're interested."

"No, I'm not ready, I don't want to die."

"Alright then, prove it to me."

"Prove...?"

"Prove it."

"How do I prove it?"

A light flashed in Sam's eyes and the vision faded out before he could even respond to the confusing question of whomever he was talking to. The light was adjusting itself and he was trying to make out certain shapes to see if he could find anything familiar. He could not but he knew he was still in the hospital. An intravenous was attached to his arm and there were a cascade of other tubes coming from his nose and mouth. He attempted to sit up but found that he was still very weak and unable to do so. He tried to speak, but only air came out, no words. He looked around to find a clock, some sort of device that would let him know the time and he finally spotted the clock on the wall. It was four in the morning. The room was a little darker now and little sound could be heard except for the shuffling of papers from the nearby nurse's station, a conversation, and the beeping of the heart monitor that he was connected to. There was another hospital bed next to him but it was unoccupied. Stacks of magazines and newspapers were on the bench by the window and he saw his mother resting there, which comforted him greatly. Part of him wanted to wake her but he knew better. The bathroom was in a room to his right and to his left, a nightstand. He lay on his side and tried to recollect what had put him into this predicament. The last thing he really remembered before the rush of calamity and a blackout was…he couldn't do it. It was all lost in the haze.

Not really surprising actually, now that he gave some

thought to it all.

He would end up in a hospital without any knowledge of how he got there. He had totally pulled a Sam, he rolled his eyes in a sort of 'typical me' manner. Not knowing what else he was to do except sleep, he did just this. He slept.

When he awoke…seven hours had passed him. There was a familiar hand on his forehead, and a not so familiar hand near his forearm.

"Sammy? Can you hear me? How ya' feelin'?"

"Dizzy," he replied softly.

"Do you need some water?"

"Yes."

His mother got up and went to the sink, filled up a Styrofoam cup of cold water and brought it to him. He still needed help sitting up to drink it. He looked to his right to make out the other person that was in the room and with one glance assumed immediately it was his doctor and he was right about this. He introduced himself as Dr. Stoermer and told Sam that he needed to run a few tests on him to see what was making him so sick. The doctor instructed one of the nurses to help Sam into his wheelchair and take him to X-ray. When Sam's feet hit the linoleum floor an instant rush of cold seized his body.

"It's cold," he said with a meek giggle.

"You want me to get you some socks?" asked Juliet.

"Yea."

Juliet got some socks for him from one of the nurses. Sam put on the wooly socks. His feet were especially cold now that he was not in the comfort of his bed anymore and further forced to put his feet on the frigid floor. Juliet tried to help him but Sam insisted on doing it himself.

He could see the worry in his mother's eyes.

"I'm not an invalid *yet* mom; I can still put on a pair of

socks." She let him be after that. Sam did this and was then helped up out of bed, something he could not yet do himself. The nurse helped him into the wheelchair, bringing him out of the room and down the hall. Sam, who wasn't all that dead this time, had more of a chance to look around for he hadn't been in a hospital since he was about five years old. The walls were whitewashed with flowery trimmed wallpaper. Carts of drugs and supplies lined the hallways, as did their managers. Nurses and staff scuttled about the floor going from task to task, patient to patient. They went onto the elevator where that classic elevator music was playing. Such music had always irritated him and he was very relieved when they got off. The nurse turned a corner and both she and Sam entered a medium-sized room with a giant vertical table. Many utensils were neatly aligned in anally retentive row. The technician helped Sam out of his chair and his mother waited outside, keeping close watch on what went on.

Then the tech assisted Sam up out of the wheelchair and onto the table, where he had to stand. Sam was handed a glass of liquid and told to drink it.

"Sam, we're going to take some pictures of your body and see if we can't pinpoint what's wrong with you. This is a special kind of machine that's going to allow us to look inside your stomach. The liquid is not going to taste the best, but I need you to push through the bitterness and drink all of it, ok?"

Sam said that he would try his best to do so and took the cup from him. He drank from it. The tech had been right, it was disgusting. It tasted like liquid bone mixed with some sort of horrid orange flavored cough medicine but Sam trooped through it. He drank the whole thing as fast as he could so he didn't have to drink the stuff anymore. He slammed the glass down when he was finished. He had a most bitter expression as if he had just drunk a bottle of vinegar. Sam stood straight up on the table just as he had been directed to and the tech took the pictures of his stomach. He felt like some sort of alien specimen the entire time, in his loose hospital gown, his ass slightly exposed, his weak bones practically protruding out of his body, with his gaunt face and both of his eyes heavy with exhaustion. Bright lights surrounded the room as he leaned up against the table. Why, the only thing missing were three or four doctors standing around him with masks on, probing him with scientific hardware and instruments used for dissecting dead bodies during autopsies. Examining him over and over, asking questions of which planet he came from and if he might be the last of his kind. He entertained the determined course of the conversation in his head to amuse and distract himself and from the uncomfortable position he was forced to be in.

"What do you reckon it is, Bob?"

"Not sure Ted, I've never seen anything like it before." Bob sipped the last of his large fast food soda from its white plastic cup.

"Maybe we should slice it open."

"What if that kills it?"

"What if it kills us first?"

"Hand me that scalpel, we'll find out for ourselves."

"You can't kill it! It's not ready to die yet."

"Well then how are we going to find out if it's friendly or not?"

"We're just going to have to give it a chance to impress us."

"It's not going to impress us; it's just another alien, from another world." Ted scratched his red head. "But whatever, we'll do this your way this time."

"Good, hand me that flashlight."

"Why?"

"Gonna take a closer look at it."

Sam playfully closed his eyes and pretended he was...but before he could decide what it was, he was snapped back to reality. The whole process took no more than half an hour and before he knew it, the tech had told him that he was ready to head back to his room. He helped him back in the wheelchair and explained that the doctor would be back to visit Sam in a day or so to tell him what he found, (if in fact he *could* find anything).

"I'm sure we'll figure this out, Sam." The tech was exceedingly reassuring as he placed his hand on Sam's shoulder and beamed a comforting smile. Sam was soon back to his hospital bed where fell noiselessly back into a perfectly sound sleep.

At this point in Sam's life, and in everyone's life I suppose, there were things that were clear, present, and known. The rain was falling hard, Sam's weight was falling faster, and there were no other people in the room with him at the moment except his mother. Sam's body was not getting any stronger and not able to sustain itself without the assistance of the intravenous tube. These were things that were known. There were other things that were murky, unclear, and unknown. What was not known to Sam was that in most normal cases of being off medication it wouldn't be a terrible problem but the combination of meds that he was on at the moment were for his ADHD and his depression. Taking one of those away for someone who had been on medication nonstop for the better part of a year, let alone someone who was not only mentally, but physically weak, was bad enough but to not be allowed either of them could prove to have very negative consequences. This, again, was something that was unknown. Sam was going on his second day without either.

That night Sam dreamed as he so often did.

Morning came too soon, accompanied by an unexpected monster.

Something didn't quite feel right, something that he couldn't put his finger on, but he felt off, he felt manic almost, like he was short fused with reality for some reason. He could not think of any reason why this was happening. When the nurse came to check on Sam as part of her morning routine, Sam tried to restrain himself from the flash of emotions that wanted to come surging out but was unable to do so. He grabbed the first thing he saw, which happened to be a bottle of water on the nightstand beside him and flung it at her as hard as he could, which sent her running out of the room. She frantically called for a doctor who immediately rushed in, surveyed what was going on and asked the nurse to go and fetch a restraint and a sedative. Stoermer repeatedly asked Sam to calm down but this only furthered his anger and Sam began yelling obscenities, for he had now run out of things to throw.

"Nurse! Nurse!" the doctor called frantically and it did not take long for one to show up.

"I need orderlies to hold this kid down, stat!"

"Do you need a sedative?"

"What the hell do you think? The kid tried to throw a book at me for God's sake! 20 cc's should be good enough."

"Right away doctor," and then she left.

Sam was delusional, going off about how the doctor just wanted to kill him and how Sam wanted him to do just that. He kept saying, "You hound! You'll be the death of me."

"Sam…I need you…to…try and calm…down." He was trying his best to restrain the child without actually hurting him but Sam was putting up quite the fight.

"Fuuuuuck!" Sam was in full hysterics at this point, crying and screaming at the top of his lungs. The doctor tried but did not have a good hold on his legs were flailing in every direction without purpose.

"I WANT TO DIE!!! I WANT TO DIE!!!" Tears were rushing out of his eyes; they couldn't last any longer trapped inside of the hurt, so they left.

The nurse came running back with the sedative unabashedly concealed within the long syringe. Seeing the needle did not help with the fact that Sam was terrified of needles. He continued to flail and twitch his limbs but the orderlies finally restrained him briefly enough to inject him with the medicine.

Even though Sam had a ton of adrenaline at the moment, medicine was prevailing and the blurs of the world slowly started surrounding him. Noises became muffled and the rage was unwillingly leaving him. The fight was being lost and Sam was going into the blackness, into that damn haze.

*Too much darkness, want to be in the light just a little longer. So sick of always being in the darkness. Too much darkn...too much dar...too mu...*and with that he was gone. He was so gone. For the next several hours he was so, so gone.

Light.

He was back.

His mom was right next to his bed.

He never wanted to close his eyes again. He felt like if he did that, he would start waking up in different countries, with different conditions being treated by different doctors. He didn't want that, he didn't want to be treated by this doctor really. He just wanted to feel all better so he could go home.

He vomited in the canister beside his bed.

The vomit was no longer the color of what he was used to seeing, that sort of monstrous, infected yellow. It had become a dark green, almost black. He didn't know what it was but the hue of it was a sight all its own. Like if a house with a wood frame and wood beams had been built by the shore of a sea and was continually battered by waves. Over time it had developed a sort of growth on it, a type of plant life and that plant life had become infected with age. That's the color it would have been, almost like dead seaweed. It was grotesque; it was a vile pile of bile.

It was bile, but Sam did not know it was bile. Funny thing, in his own body and he didn't know what it was. *Ain't that a kick in the head?*

It was a sick and slimy substance to look at and the sight made him retch. Outside of his room he heard a nurse about ready to come in, but she had been stopped by another staff member and the two were now having a conversation about something medical-related. Sam did not know nor did he care. He assumed that she would come in and ask him what the stuff he just projected out of himself might be and why it was there. He wouldn't know this, he wasn't the expert, he was the patient; the sick skinny kid patient. Sam thought for a moment and decided he was first of all too weak to think anymore and certainly too weak to answer any questions with big words in them. That was most likely the kind that were going to be fired in his direction when the nurse came in to check on him. He decided to play dead when she came in. He just wanted to be left alone for goodness sake. Too many people, too many problems and he figured pretending to be asleep might avert him the headache of a conversation. So with that he closed his eyes and faked rest.

The nurse clicked her way on into the room with her clipboard cradled in her arms like a child. She was close to his bed when Sam heard a faint gasp escape her and he figured she had seen what was in the bucket. He paid her shock no attention, he continued to fake sleep. She swiftly went out of the room, minutes later she returned with a doctor that was not his own.

"What's the kid's name?"

"Sam, Sam Reed."

Sam felt a hand on his shoulder that began to softly rock him back to their reality.

"Sam, Sam, can you wake up for me please?"

Sam didn't think that they were going to give this up so for the sake of not wasting time, he rolled over and opened his eyes.

"What is it?" he tried to act like they had woken him up from a very important nap.

"We're here to talk about what's going on with you, Sam."

"Do you know what's wrong with me?"

"No, we don't. The one thing we know is that it's a very serious strain of virus. There was another kid a few years older than you who had something similar but he didn't..."

"He didn't what?" Sam was no longer off in another land, the doctor had his full attention and his speech was stern.

"It's not to say that the same thing is going to happen to you but if it is the same virus then we need to treat it the same way." He pulled the bucket from underneath Sam's bed and showed him. It made Sam furl up a bit.

"Do you know what that is, Sam?"

Sam thought that this might be a trick question. *Well it sure as hell ain't chocolate milk.* "Vomit?" he replied

"Well yes, but it's more than that." He said this like he was selling something on an infomercial, like maybe the cell phone being sold was also a blender. *But it's so much more than that!*

"It's called bile, Sam, and it's a substance what your body throws up when it has nothing left inside of it. Sort of like a last resort."

"Last resort before what?" said Sam, rightfully worried. "I'm guessing that's a bad thing."

"Well it's certainly not a good thing. It would help if you could try and eat something, even if you throw it right back up at least we'll know you tried."

Sam nodded in agreement.

"I'll have the nurse here go and fetch you a menu so you can take a look and decide if there's anything on there that you think you might be able you handle."

He looked at the nurse as he said this who took this as her cue to go and do what the doctor had just said. Sam didn't even really have anything to say, it all sounded good to him so he just continued to nod his head.

The nurse came back a few minutes after she had left to get a menu for Sam. She handed it over to him and smiled. Sam in turn smiled back. Looking over the menu, he immediately picked out Jell-O, something that could cure most ailments, and hopefully that included whatever Sam had. The nurse left only briefly to retrieve the tiny clear plastic container with its red, sticky, and wiggly substance from a cabinet in the back of the nurses' storage room. She brought it back to him; smile still plastered on her face, and handed it to him. Sam finished in a matter of seconds and when he was done the nurse threw the remnants in the trash and asked if there was anything else she could get him. Affectionately he looked into her waiting eyes and said, "Better."

A wave of sympathy flooded over her face as she looked at the child's uncertain expression. All she could do in such a situation was smile more. There was unease about the way she was looking at him, perhaps she knew something he did not and this mystery worried Sam, the worry showed because the nurse knelt down by Sam's bedside and put her hand on his forehead.

"I bet this is scary for you, isn't it?"

Sam fully agreed but did not say so, instead he asked a question. "What do you tell someone when you know they're going to die?"

The nurse was puzzled that such a question was being asked of such a young person. "Do you think you're going to die?"

Sam grappled with this for a moment before looking back with a "yes, I do" and it was the truth. He truly felt he might.

She said nothing for a second or two before finding the appropriate statement to break the uncomfortable silence. "Well I'm here to make sure that doesn't happen to you."

"What if it does?" a solitary tear was building up in his eye.

"It's not going to. You need to rest now; you need to get your strength for tomorrow." And with that, she left him with one last reassuring smile, though he was far from reassured, he felt convinced. Maybe he was going to be okay but maybe he might not make it and the nurse had just told him something to help him go to sleep. Whether or not it was true, it was nonetheless convincing and that helped. Sam looked outside of the glossy hospital window where it was nighttime outside.

It was raining very hard when Sam closed his eyes and his mind began to empty itself.

In the next three days, Sam's condition began to steadily decline but not to the point where family or friends needed to be notified. Intravenous was still his main source of nutrition though he was still able to keep down Jell-O just not as much as he would have liked. His mother continued to keep watch over him for the majority of the time but his grandparents would step in for her when she needed rest or had to run errands. Nights and mornings were a particularly difficult time for him and that's when he needed company the most. The nurses always kept Sam entertained with stories and movies to keep his mind off the fact that his body was beginning to give up the fight. Sam was thirteen years old, approximately 5'7, and he weighed 95 pounds. His family had told the staff not to tell him what his weight was but Sam knew it was at a very unhealthy level. Still, he didn't say anything about it. He knew. His mother would worry if she knew he knew, he just felt she had enough on her plate as it was.

As it was.

As it was he wanted to sleep, but figured he would do so when he was dead. Wasn't too far off was it? Nah, it shouldn't be at this point. He was almost to the point of giving up hope...

He threw up more bile.

...but something told him to hang on a little longer and as weak as he was, as much as wanted to let this virus have him forever and be done with it, be done with the bullying, be done with the hound who was crouched patiently outside...he told himself he would hold on for one more day. If he was no better in twenty-four hours then he would stop caring and let whatever happened, happen.

That night he stepped into another universe yet again and dreamed. He dreamed he was in a palace wearing what seemed to be a black cloth draped over his shoulders with dirty brown sandals that had more than begun to fall apart. He was also strapped to his hospital bed in the middle of what seemed to be the main room. He leaned over to the side of the bed where...

"It's you again!" he said, frightened.

"Ah, so now you recognize me."

"Why are you here? Why am I here? Why is...that...here?" Sam pointed to the hound who was sitting in the corner of the palace, glancing over at him and eating a fresh rack of lamb; a bottle of red wine sat beside him.

"You're not doing a very good job of taking my advice, Sam."

"What advice?"

"I told you to prove it. You don't seem to be proving anything other than the fact that you don't want this anymore."

"Don't want what?"

"Life."

"What exactly can *you* do about that?"

"I can take it away from you."

"Why would you do a thing like that?" Sam fixed his face now from new fear to curious frustration.

"Why wouldn't we? Haven't seen you put forth much effort into wanting to survive. How about I let the old hound pull the plug on ya, eh?"

"No! I don't want that devil near me."

"Oh Samuel," the hound piped up finally after being silent this whole time, walking on the glass floor. "Don't be so spiteful. We're only here to make a deal with you."

"You just want me dead." He was getting cold. "You keep away from me!"

"Calm down, Samuel don't make this something that's going to be painful." The man, Sam still didn't know who he was, was wearing a white, three-piece suit and held a full syringe in his hand. There was a tiny bottle on the white wood nightstand next to him marked 'fear me' and the seal had been broken. Sam knew that must be what was inside the needle.

"Here's what's going to happen, Samuel. I'm going to give you two options."

Sam looked past the mask and into the man's eyes. They were cold and untrustworthy and he knew better than to listen to anything he was saying.

"The first thing I will do is to loosen these straps and let you free. If you can make it past the hound and through those doors I'll let you live. However if the hound corners you and you cannot win then I'm going to give you to him and let him have his way with you. Does that sound fair?"

"Fine." Sam knew he must have been dreaming, otherwise he certainly would not have answered so nonchalantly.

The man in white let Sam go, and still in his dream he walked, almost floated, to the middle of the room where a giant circular emblem was cast.

The hound put its glass of wine down on the floor and walked over to where Sam was, its teeth stained with lamb it had just eaten.

"Do you know what it's like to die, Samuel Reed?" The hound's stare seemed to go straight through Sam the entire time. Sam tried to remind himself that this was only a dream but for him it had surpassed that. This was not something he wanted to shake himself from. He didn't want to wake up from this particular nightmare, not this time. He wanted to do what he had always wanted to do with his fears. He wanted to grapple them to the ground and defeat them. This hound had brought him nothing but distress for the better part of the last two years and it was time Sam Reed stood up and faced his demon in the eye.

"I promise I won't be as forgiving as I was last time."

"I don't expect your fraudulent forgiveness, or your seemingly intimidating words. I expect you to go away."

"You're funny, but I'm not going to do that."

Sam was done playing around. He had no fear in his eyes and in fact no emotion whatsoever and this made him sense for the first time that the hound was uneasy.

"I'm not afraid of you."

"You are though, I can smell it." The hound was

starting to worry but tried to hide it, like Sam had tried to once hide his panic when *that bitch* had soiled the hallways of his school with those words. Sam saw the fear. He saw something that he was supposed to be afraid of, fearing him. And he thought it was about time.

"No, you're afraid of me." He spoke the truth with a vengeance.

"I fear nothing. I am every drop of blood that has left your body when you cut yourself on steel. I am the shadow in the corner of your room that doesn't waver with the wind. I am the noise in your ear that tells you that when you close your eyes you'll never wake up again…"

No you're not, I've seen Satan, and you're just a pawn, a nothing, a nobody like me. "I've heard enough!" Sam yelled this across the room, so loudly in fact that it shook the building and everything in it. The diamonds on the chandelier rattled and tiny cracks were visible on the marble floor. The hound was shaking and shrinking.

"I know what you are…"

The hound barked.

"…and you have no power over me anymore."

And with those very words, mighty indeed, the hound screeched, not barked but screeched, like a harpy would screech. Its mouth gaped open into an unworldly black hole. Its silver, knife-lined mouth exposed sights of torture and pestilence; decaying bodies being whipped to death without dying, their brains and insides being devoured by snakes and spiders. Hailstones of fire rained from the sky and people moaned as they clawed their way through cold mud and hot brimstone.

Sam just shook his head. "Back to your playground," he said, and with that, Sam turned his back on the beast.

The hound's eyes froze with the rest of its body, its black luster faded and its tail curled in between its legs. Its mouth closed and the horrors it had so proudly displayed were gone instantly. Then without any last sounds, the hound sank into an expanding puddle of blood on the ground. Dark, wet, red blood oozed all around and the beast twisted and mutated into a gross splotch of nothing. He then turned his attention to the man in the corner of the room that had been silently watching, not moving or saying a thing.

"Now let me out," said Sam, a deadly seriousness seething from his voice and the man in white took out a white pistol and shot himself point blank in the face, vanishing in a cloud of silver haze, similar to what the hound had been born in.

The doors opened, a flash of light came from them and Sam went through those large wooden doors and back into somewhere.

He woke up.

It was morning, 9am to be exact. He blinked his eyes a few times and got the crust out that had lodged itself in the far corner of his left eye. The sun was shining through the windowpane with no daily illuminating metaphors. It just shone like it was supposed to be doing. His mother was on the bench near the window reading a book. She glanced over and saw that he was awake, came over, and kissed him on the forehead.

He returned her warm concern with a welcome beam. He looked at his arms where the tubes continued to provide nourishment and a misplaced sense of optimism. The nurse was on the other side of the room washing her hands thoroughly and with care. A plate of breakfast was dished on a tray table beside his bed. Cheerios. He examined the meager feast with something he hadn't felt in a while; the instinct of hunger and want. He used his arms, which now resembled small twigs and pushed up with everything he had but doing so carefully in fear of breaking them, and sat himself upright in his bed. The nurse heard him stirring about in his bed and happily came to his assistance. Her happiness took nothing from the pleasantry of her company. Sam was in fact, happy to see her.

"Do you want me to bring your tray table closer to you?" she asked

"Yes, please." Sam said. The nurse noticed him wearing a new found glow.

"You're looking much improved today. Are you feeling better?"

"I feel much better, thank you."

"Good! Do you think you can eat breakfast this morning?" she brought the tray table closer to him, unwrapped the Cheerios from their white packet and poured them into the tiny blue hospital bowl. She placed in it a tiny, white plastic spoon. Sam looked up and said thanks as though she had just performed some sort of astounding public service. He could not contain his eagerness to eat, and they were Cheerios for goodness sake. Cheerios! The saliva was dripping down from his mouth as if he was getting chocolate chip pancakes but it was just a little bowl of those classically dull whole wheat O's floating around aimlessly in his hospital brand whole milk. The nurse left Sam with his breakfast. He picked up his spoon, dunked it in the bowl of cereal and took a bite. His mother, now at his side, beamed at this encouraging sight.

Sam was feeling feelings he shouldn't have felt over a bowl of cereal but the taste of anything in his mouth again was ecstasy. He made a groaning sound and his eyes rolled halfway up. A few more enthusiastic bites and everything was finished. Now, he sat and waited. Waited for all of that effort and hunger to be in vain. First five minutes, then fifteen, then a half an hour went by and Sam had thrown nothing up. He drank some orange juice; same story, nothing came up. Being one such person to put the cart before the horse, Sam decided that since he could keep a bowl of Cheerios and a glass of orange juice down, that he was all of a sudden ready to walk after being confined to a bed for a little over a week.

"You're rushing things a bit, don't you think?" His mother was still there, he had almost forgotten. The ADHD was kicking in though and Sam wanted to move now.

"Maybe you should wait a while and then slowly ease into it." Her advice was welcomed but not obeyed. Sam was ready; even if his body wasn't, his mind was.

"Well, let me go get the I.V. pole." Juliet grabbed the wheeled pole and brought it over beside the bed, helping Sam up slowly onto the white linoleum floor.

"Ok now Sam," his mom addressed him in a serious tone. "Don't rush anything, take your time, just because you feel better doesn't mean you *are* better." She was in full mother mode. Sam grabbed the I.V. pole and slowly but surely raised himself up out of bed.

One foot on the floor at a time, then it was both feet taking steps, one step at a time. He was walking, and his legs, along with the rest of him, were operable. He still required some assistance, but he was walking nonetheless.

The nurse had him walk over to the scale, and for the first time in a long time, he saw his actual weight.

It read 120.

His mother smiled honestly at him, her contagious optimism resonating through her eyes.

Sam knew he was going to be just fine.

The terrible illness and the swift recovery that followed it were never completely diagnosed. The majority of responses he heard from the floor staff was that he was a very lucky kid. All Sam knew was one day he was vomiting his life away, the next he was close to death, and then one day he woke up to find that whatever had been ravaging through him had moved on to something or someone else. He looked up towards the sky as he exited the hospital and whispered under his breath, "I don't know what your deal is…but thank you."

Then the kid who beat death left with his mom to go home.

Now some people would expect things to only look up for Sam being as all he had put up with at this point. To some extent it was like that, but it wasn't an easy battle still being the outcast. Though his days as a hospitalized invalid were at an end, continual name-calling and harassment never saw an end to their long lived days and it was especially bad now that the fourteen year-old was entering his first year of high school. The unfamiliar halls that he would roam for the next five years, for he would be held back for another year, reminded him of The Overlook Hotel though much smaller. They were long and narrow yet more generous, foreboding but seemingly safe at first glance. The withstanding walls and trophies held safely within the confines of their glass houses, some were new and gleaming others were unpolished and forgotten like the former stars who had once earned them. The intimidation of it all was overwhelming at first but he just numbed himself to everything and pressed on.

High school was a joke, the whole shebang. Though it wasn't necessarily a waste of time, it was something that he could have done without. The first two years of it were particularly grueling, especially Freshman year when he had been duct taped to the wall of the boys' locker room one day with 'fag' written on the tape in black sharpie. But aside from that, still not fitting in was the same story. It was nothing close to an innocent prank in their eyes and Sam would never be comfortable going into a locker room again because of it. That made the gym class he was in particularly difficult. He would always walk fast across the faded white and blue ceramic tiles to the nearest stall, change there, and exit as swiftly as he had entered paying no attention to anyone else...especially since many of them he had known from middle school and the "incident" that he had with that girl...

Bitch, she was a bitch, remember?

...that had done him the liberty of announcing his predetermined sexual orientation to the entire school. His ears were still swelling from the poison.

"Hey everyone..."

The echo still made him flinch from time to time.

"Sam Reed is gay!"

If he had been at the point of caring, he would have surely felt the rain coming on, but he wasn't in the habit of feeling much anymore. He walked the halls and he felt some stares but, whatever. He was a nobody and that was fine with him, as long as he continued to be a nobody who got an equal amount of nobody attention. Sophomore year, everyone started getting their license and driving but Sam. His maturity level was five years behind what it should be and therefore he would not be driving for many, many years. Not that any of this mattered to him. He become so accustomed to walking everywhere that driving would just feel weird to him.

In the anticlimactic transition between being an underclassman to an upperclassman, his friends remained relatively the same and he was also making new ones fairly well. He was still in his high school state of wanting to fit in and who was to say that was something that was going to change. Nearly everyone in high school wanted that feeling of belonging, even the kids who seemed like they had it all, and Sam was no exception. His focus on finding a girlfriend to charade his obvious homosexuality was a lost cause and he knew it but he thought 'what the hell' and decided to give it one final attempt. Whether he disappointed himself with failure or managed to blossom an actual steady relationship, either way, he didn't care. It was half wanting someone to be with and half wanting to prove that he was just as normal as everyone else. Wanting to prove one's normalcy in high school was further proof that you are anything but.

Ruby, like the gemstone she was, was once a quiet corner mouse who was now finding her way out of her shell and becoming more and more outspoken. She had wavy auburn blonde hair that stretched down almost to her elbows. Her petite frame and blue eyes were especially stunning, but her participation in the arts kept her under the radar of preps. What caught Sam's attention the most though was her extinguishable sense of humor which was one he could relate to. He thought that even if he didn't get to be with her, she would at least be able to understand him.

Sam was sitting in his sophomore world history class one day looking out of the window at the light on the windowpane and wishing he was outside playing in the sun. This was stealing his attention from the lesson his teacher was rambling on about; something about the downfall of the Roman Empire, information that was important for an upcoming test, but his mind was focused on the other things going on around him. There was a group of boys outside the door who were conversing about what the girl in their chemistry class had said to one of them, the girl next to him was filing her nails, and in the classroom next to them there was a movie playing but Sam could not figure out which one it was. Now, all of these things may seem silly things to devote attention to, but keep in mind that Sam's brain was a brain that worked much differently from most people's brains. While the other kids in the class could simply shut these sounds out and listen, Sam's brain could not differentiate between information that was relevant and information that was not. So Mr. Bombson's cloying talk on test material was just as important as the girl next to him who had put away her nail file and was now applying lip gloss. Mr. Bombson threw a pencil at her head to get her attention. The class laughed, and Sam was grateful that he didn't get a pencil thrown at him. He was sure he was going to fail the test anyway and saw no point in writing anything down. Sam just continued to impatiently jiggle his legs, ennui, waiting for this class to be over. Classes were just mediocre for Sam and he had developed a pattern for them from the very beginning. If the subject AND the teacher engaged him and squeezed onto his attention then he excelled and gave all of himself toward working for a good grade. If the subject OR the teacher was interesting to him, then he would absorb the information but end up barely passing if not failing the class. It was a simple process. Sam put into the class and teacher what they put into him, and his grades suffered tremendously because of it. It was all a matter of interest, really. If there was a subject that really piqued his interest and the teacher taught it well then he would excel. Likewise, if a subject couldn't hold his attention, he would not care and wind up failing it. Sam was unusually content with this pattern even if his mother and teachers were not.

When the bell finally rang signaling the end of the period, he fast walked to the school's coffee stand to buy coffee for Ruby in hopes of winning her heart. A favorite of hers that she had mentioned to him earlier that day before they had started their theater class together was a white chocolate raspberry mocha. He wrote the message asking her to be his girlfriend on the side of the cup, walked to her class and waited for her to get out. When the door opened, Sam saw Ruby and they locked eyes. Ruby grabbed her bag and made her way over to Sam.

"Heeeyyy," Ruby said with a soft, mellow smile.

"Hey Ruby, how was class?"

"Eh, it was *a'ight*." she looked down at the cup in his hands. "You *has* coffee."

"I does. Actually, this is for you…actually." He winced at the misconstruction and handed her the cup.

"Aww, my favorite! I can't believe you remembered."

"What do you mean? You told me this morning."

"My point exactly." She looked at him in a 'duh I was kidding' look and smiled, He got the joke.

They both laughed at this and walked down the hall talking about an assignment that was due soon for the theater class they both shared. They had to memorize and recite a line from Hamlet.

Speak the speech I pray thee, as I pronounce it to you know trippingly on the tongue. But if you mouth it, as many of your players do, I had as leif the town crier spoke my lines.

They shot the phrase back and forth to each other for a while and kept on walking. Ruby was trying to distract Sam with the assignment in hopes that he might forget the real reason as to why he was walking her to lunch, but, to no avail, he remembered.

"So, Ruby, I've been wondering something."

"Yea?" She asked, trying to sound curious but actually was more sad because she knew the question and knew even better what her response was going to be. She liked Sam, but knew without a doubt that he was gay. She had remembered the first time she saw him walking down the hallway. They had not even met yet but smiled cordially at each other. Ruby turned around long enough to see him strut in the opposite direction and thought to herself, "yep, that one's gay," the hard part now was helping Sam see the same inevitable revelation.

"Will you…

He paused only once.

...be my girlfriend?"

Sam's hazel hued eyes collided with Ruby's baby blues as he said this and his sweet charm mixed with such a sincere certainty that he really did love her made Ruby, in that moment anyway, want to throw her arms around him and irrevocably say "Yes, Oh! Yes!" She caught herself though and her face changed from a smile to...the look. That unwanted heartbroken expression when every girl has to tell her gay friend that they're gay, because he doesn't even know it himself. Sam had never even kissed a boy so his sexuality, though chosen, had yet to be solidified.

"Baby," she echoed out her disappointment, and Sam sensed it right away, looking down at the ground, awaiting the anticipated rejection.

"I can't." She would not tell him why, other than she just didn't really want a boyfriend and Sam, being not the kind of guy to push anything on anybody, let it die immediately.

"Oh, ok," he said, broken but putting on a happy face.

Almost as if he were trying to tell her that she was just the first in many other girls that were single, attractive, and ready and raring to deny his propositions of love.

"Can I at least walk you to lunch?"

"Absolutely." She took his arm, and they walked off towards the cafeteria. Sam was never one to eat in there, due to too many people in there who wanted to beat him up; but if Ruby wanted to, he would make a special exception, just this one time. For a friend.

Sam looked outside, there was a cloud covering the sun but other than that, it was a beautiful day.

He blinked, and the cloud was gone, as was the school year and its challenges. Ruby kept in contact with Sam that summer and the two began to cultivate their remarkable friendship. It was one of many unforgettable friendships he would be making in the next year, some with brighter stories, and others with more interesting beginnings.

The summer of 2005 was one such season that would
begin brightly, get darker, and brighten up again in the end.
Sam had heard from a friend he had met in a local coffee
shop that a local theater guild located south of Lynville was
in need of someone to work with the lighting for the play
and was willing to pay cash. Being unemployed, Sam's
mother still supplied all of his needs but he went to the
auditions anyway even though he had no intention of
performing. He was a natural on the stage but suffered from
severe stage fright and did not like being in large crowds of
people. His ADHD went into overload mode and started
looking at everything. That's when he would become
overwhelmed. Long story short, he shied away from being
on stage as much as he wanted to be on one. When his
mom dropped him off at the house where the auditions
were taking place, he quickly realized everyone else in the
group had met before with the exception of Sam who knew
nobody. He was simply branching himself out to try
something new and adventurous.

By so doing, he met a warm hearted, kindred spirit who
knew rejection's familiar sting, and immediately embraced
her. Abigail Shalot was a tall but shapely young girl with
short brown hair and vivid blue and green eyes; just a young
and scared girl with hardly any friends to speak of, and no
future beyond the front doors of her own home. Until, of
course, she met Sam. Their personalities attracted each
other instantly and they knew a friendship was going to
ensue, but the power of the friendship was still somewhat
unknown to both. Sam exuded the same sort of fear (or
maybe it was just nerves). They couldn't really tell but they
clicked almost immediately. Introductions went around the

room and once everyone had auditioned, the director of the play, a middle-aged woman, turned to Sam and asked him if he would like to audition for any real parts. Being as he was getting paid for this, he wanted to say no but the craving for the stage compelled him to say yes.

There was no denying that Sam loved being the center of attention. Even at this new level in life, where he was still sort of entering into his new cocoon of ostentatious flamboyancy and attraction to stardust and anything sequined. Sam had his fantasies of wearing a floor length, blood red, Oscar de la Renta gown with dazzling diamonds cascading down his neck with matching chandelier earrings; white satin elbow length gloves on both hands and makeup from eyelid to eyelid performing Cabaret carte blanche without a flaw, in front of a sold out crowd at Carnegie Hall. The feeling of the satin on his skin, the juicy matching blood-red lipstick shimmering on his mouth, as the hot spotlight illuminating his blushed face. The power of each note being belted from his diaphragm as the crowd ooh-ed and aah-ed, overcome with wonderment.

"It's gunnaa haappen!! Haappen sometiiime! Maayyybee thiis tiiime I'll Wiiiiiiiiiiiiiiiiiiiiiiiiiiiiiiiiiiiiiiiiiiiiiiiiiiiinnnnnnn!!"

And the applause, the roar of the applause would rise from the seats, and roses would adorn the stage. Nothing could compare to this sound; it was the sound of love, of acceptance, encouragement, and of utter adoration. It was a sound Sam wanted to fill his ears with so much. The women would run toward him in a brisk fever of joy, trying to keep the feathers in their hair and cocktail rings from falling off their fingers just so they could ask him where he learned to dress like this and sing like that. Men dressed in tuxes, silk top hats, and gold pocket watches would talk in groups about him but would not be able to speak a single foul word. They would speak just like the police did that found him dead in his head so long ago.

See that Samuel Reed there on that stage, he may be queer but damn, he put on one hell of a performance, didn't he? That kid went out with a bang, he did.

All these self-produced accolades sent him into a heavenly orbit. But fantasies are just this, dreams that will never leave the encompassment of the mind. Someday though, someday, he would win, and big.

Sam auditioned for the play with no such fabulous regalia or spotlights; he just played the part simply and ended up getting one of the male leads.

When the first day of practice came, Sam and Abigail spent the majority of their time joking around like old pals who had gone back further than their lives on Earth. What Sam didn't know was that Abigail had taken a very strong liking to Sam, and wanted Sam to take similar interest in her. As the play went on and practices transformed into performances, Abigail found that that they were becoming closer every time they saw each other. Abigail's mom, a strong woman very similar to her daughter, would pick Sam up everyday to carpool to the church where the production was being held. Until one day something changed...in Sam.

Something that Abigail didn't really know what to put her finger on. Sam had begun acting in a way that was unfamiliar in her. Later she would end up referring to it as "flamboyant" but all she continually saw in the overly hyper boy was the same heartbreak that she herself had experienced. Sam understood her in ways that not a lot of people did. A few days before their last production, it was Abigail's birthday, which happened to be three days before Sam's birthday, so Abigail's parents had planned a combined birthday party. Sam would be turning seventeen, Abigail, fifteen. There was a multitude of food. Everyone from the play and a few of Abi's other friends had joined them as well, but Sam and his now overly social self had no problem introducing himself to new people.

Sam had brought over the movie "Big Fish," one of his all time favorites and during the film Sam laid his head on Abi's lap, something that she did not understand; she did not understand a lot of how or why right now anyway. Sam was naturally a touchy-feely person and overly affectionate to most everyone. In his perpetual state of ADHD, he did not realize that everyone else did not act the same way and felt this was appropriate and socially acceptable behavior. Shortly after the movie, Sam said goodbye to Abi. Her mom gave him a ride home. Then—the phone call.

Fort whatever reason, Sam had called Abigail when he had gotten home and he sounded extremely distressed.

"Sam, calm down, what's going on?"

"I have to tell you something."

"What is it?" Abigail was waiting for something though she wasn't sure what, but nothing shocked her as much as what Sam said to her next.

"Abi…I'm gay."

Her mind went blank.

"I'm seeing somebody right now," he continued.

Abi was so unsure how to take any of it. She responded with the only words that her mind would let her use. "Sam, I still love you." She heard herself say this on the other end. "I will still be your friend no matter what."

In that moment Sam not only realized what he had said but what Abigail's true feelings of him had been virtually the whole time they had known each other. They ended the phone conversation, both still not knowing how to handle what had just happened. Abigail had been bound in even tighter chains of religious upbringing than Sam and didn't know what being gay really meant. The term had been familiar to her before but she didn't really know what all that entailed. Naturally, her parents were not happy that she had found out, and heavily expressed it through their anger.

So much so, that she was not allowed to see Sam until things had cooled down a bit. When Sam came over next it was more to apologize with a member of the church he was attending at the time, he gave an excellent half-assed speech about love and forgiveness in cases of homosexuality. Sam cried. Abigail cried.

After that was all over, they didn't see much of each other, and missed each other terribly until one day Abigail got a call from Sam saying that he would be reciting some poetry at a local coffee shop. Abigail wasn't allowed to go unless she got a ride, so she was accompanied that night by her mother.

Sam had had a lot of coffee that night and was having immense issues sitting still. He had not taken his medication for his ADHD either, so his brain felt like highways and byways of speeding cars, intersections of green light thoughts, and car crashes of ideas and things he had remembered from eight years ago. For Sam, it was like trying to look at every boxcar on two speeding trains going the opposite way and feeling like you needed to remember what each and every one looked like. It simply wasn't a good night to be making a more appropriate second impression on anyone, let alone Abi's mother and that was about to be made very clear with almost irreversible consequences.

As hyper and uncontrollable as he felt, Sam performed his poetry magnificently and Abigail felt the connection of two lovely souls spark up again just like old times. But just when things were going good, the two trains got caught on the same track and collided. Sam was literally so excited and hyperactive, not to mention still trying to function without the assistance of medication and filled with coffee, that he literally peed himself and out of what seemed to have been half nervousness and half the ADHD, he took a jacket from Abi's mother's van not knowing what it was and rubbed it all over his groin, throwing it back at her when he was done.

His mind created the thunderstorm.

An unforgivable mix of horror and anger spread across her face that made her look like she may have been able to produce lightning. Sam turned away from her like he had done nothing wrong. His brain hadn't even had time to tell him that he had just made a huge mistake. In fact the impulse had been blocked, restricted even, and Sam was not aware that he had done anything offensive. It was this fact that horrified Abi's mother into leaving immediately. She herded the two kids into the van and dropped Sam off at home like nothing had happened. Goodbyes and everything were spoken; after that night, Abigail's mother told her daughter that she was never to see the likes of that boy ever again, and it seemed that the friendship was over almost as quickly as it had begun.

Their friendship was like a vase that had been dropped not too far from the ground but far enough to break. The pieces were fairly big but some were very small and unrecognizable. It would take a while to fit it all back together. They wouldn't see each other again for another four years.

It was clear to Sam that his ADHD was out of control and at this point. Taking his medication would have been the wisest thing to do, but there was a part of his mind that wanted independence, and resisted the thought of taking any drugs. He ultimately decided to do things its own way.

The church he was currently attending had been raising money for a mission trip to Mexico. Sam had every intention of going on it but he wanted to be off of his medicine while he was away. When he visited his doctor he heard an unsatisfying story.

"I can't do that Sam."

"Why not!?" Sam expressed his frustration with the meds.

"If I was to suddenly take you off this medicine or if

you were to stop taking it, your brain would suddenly be denied chemicals that it has become dependant on almost six years. That could have terrible negative consequences."

"Like what?"

"ADHD could become unmanageable, your depression could also worsen, and you may even become suicidal."

"That's it, huh?" Sam said, sarcastically.

"Yea, that's all."

He nodded his head and assured his doctor that he would continue with his medication. Sam was already lying about many things, small in severity but numerous. He didn't know it at the time but it was all due to his ADHD and his brain's constant need for stimulation. Sam thought none of this could possibly happen to him and the day he left for Mexico, he took his medicine container with him, no intention of taking one pill, and he would pay for it dearly, almost with his life, but more so with his mind.

Tijuana was a populated but run down city. Multi-colored shacks littered its hilltops which overlooked a beautiful but polluted Pacific Ocean. The crew had been advised not to go swimming in the ocean at risk of contracting worms. Battered streets and fenced off alleyways were teeming with stray dogs wandering through merchant bartering kiosks and straw markets. Despite being run down and poverty stricken it was a colorful country with delicious food and vibrant culture.

The aim of their trip was to visit a tiny village outside of Tijuana and help build two houses for two families in need, something that Sam was very excited about. Helping people had always made him happy and helping those who were less fortunate was especially satisfying to him. Though he was now a deteriorating Christian, he held on to his values with the utmost conviction.

The day started normal. Sam ate breakfast with a small group of friends. The youth leader that his mom had told to keep an eye on him approached Sam and asked him if he had taken his pills yet.

"Not yet, I need to eat something first."

"Ok, well just make sure you take them."

Sam didn't bother with this; he simply wasn't going to take them. Sam didn't wanna be on medication anymore and he felt he was old and mature enough to sever the relationship he had with pills.

He sat at the table, his mind floating around aimlessly like the Cheerios that were in his bowl. Cheerios. That cute little jingle that went with it. *The whuun and ohhn-lyy Cheer-i-ohhs.*

He laughed at this. He didn't know why this particular memory had been snatched from the fish tank either but he just remembered how they had been the first food he had been able to keep down when he was in the hospital, recovering from…whatever it was that he had been stricken with. That had been almost four years ago now. Four years ago he had been threatened by the hound, which he had not seen since. He hadn't really seen a whole lot of darkness. Strangely enough, though his life was much less dark now it was also much less eventful. Sure, he was in Mexico and having a great time there but at least when there was darkness he felt like he was paid a little more attention to. As negative as that attention was, he was still being recognized as living. Now he was just another kid lost in a crowd of faces. Sam didn't know why he clung on to the darkness. It was something he repelled yet magnetized to at the same time.

The rest of the group had started packing up and the leaders loaded groups into two separate vans of groups. It was about 10:00 or so in the morning and it was already very hot. The sun was not even directly overhead then, and the oily sweat was like glitter on everyone's forehead. Their destination was almost in the middle of the desert on the outskirts of a town that was even smaller than where they had been based. Mounds that resembled small cliffs of dry, orange dirt broke out of the ground and stretched outward for miles but wasn't incredibly high. The place was darn near deserted except for a couple of shacks with woven rugs draped over the opening where the door was supposed to be. They had patterns that were reminiscent of something the early Native Americans would have made.

The team was greeted at the entryway by a tiny-framed but friendly Mexican woman who told them where they would be building the houses (the whole reason the team had come to Mexico in the first place) and saw that everything they needed had already been brought. A table of power tools, paint canisters, brushes, hammers, nails, and a variety of hardware equipment was laid out before them. Sam who was dead set on not even looking at a power saw. He would not even want to go near one if he even knew *how* to operate one. He immediately went for the paintbrushes and grabbed a can of the pink paint. The other can was green but had been snatched already. A few other girls grabbed their own brushes as well and followed him to the frame of the plywood structure. A few trusses were laid out in front of them and they began painting. Sam looked over and saw one of the power saws buzz over a piece of wood slicing it into quarters. He tensed up; he didn't like sharp fast moving objects. He was very happy with just painting.

Not even thirty minutes into what he had been doing Sam looked up and noticed just how much fun it would be to play around in the dirt but was only slightly worried that this might look a little childish to everyone else who didn't have the imagination and childlike mind that Sam had. Nonetheless, he was bored with just painting. It was so repetitive. Dip, shake, and glide. Painting reminded him of one time in kindergarten the class had been learning about mixing different primary colors to make new secondary ones. Red and yellow made orange, red and blue made violet, and yellow and blue made green. Sam had mixed all of them together and made black, which he splattered all over the easel because he wanted to make an explosion and he certainly did. He thought it was pretty cool, his teacher and the roll of paper towels it took to clean up the paint that landed everywhere but on the canvas, did not.

He was already getting bored and wanted something else to do but he could go nowhere. Jittery and distracted the rest of the day, he got little done and was scowled at by most of his team.

He couldn't control it!

Lies. He knew he could have, he should have taken his damn medication so he wouldn't be such a…how had his second grade teacher put it again? Oh yes…*rambunctious ball of fail,"* that's the one. When one is called so many vibrant names it's very difficult to keep up with the most creative and colorful. Rambunctious ball of fail had been original, as had faggot at one point, but kids wore it out fast like an eight year old boy wears out jeans with holes and grass stains. He floated on with his thoughts.

I wish I was playing in the grass, with my soccer ball, kicking it around and into my grandma's garden where she would come out and yell at me, "Stay outta my flowerbed." All while she made me lunch, ham and cheese with lettuce on a whole wheat bun. I would still play in the dirt a little bit and maybe look at the bugs flying around.

Sam was still a little kid at heart and his wanting to play with dirt was more of a way to help him think than anything else. It channeled all the activity going on in his brain to whatever he was fiddling with in his hands. The same reason he kicked and swished around in puddles. It wasn't for recreation; it was his way of saying, "I'm thinking, come back to me later with your questions and sandwiches."

The sun was so incredibly bright as it sizzled the earth below Sam's feet. He felt as though Lee Renwick might come back from the dead just so he could duel on such a day. Sam would whip out his pistol before Lee could breathe but he would dodge it somehow and the two would be locked in a battle for blood while the vultures made their circles in the sky above them, looking on with eager anticipation for fresh carrion. Sam could almost hear the saloon piano suddenly stop as whiskey bottles and glasses of beer were lowered, heads poked outside of the swinging wooden doors to see the fight that...

"Sam! We need you help over here."

A voice broke this movie reel of images he had playing and focused his attention where it should have been the entire time, doing his job. It was one of the leaders. He had somehow strayed about fifty yards away and was being motioned back. He ran over to see what he had been needed for, most likely help packing supplies up. Work, work, work that's all they seemed to do. Why couldn't everyone be as carefree as he was?

"Time to head out," was all they said.

Trust me; I headed out of this desert long before we arrived. I headed waaay out. His mind already wanted to be somewhere else that wasn't where it was supposed to be.

"Where were you this whole time?" said one of the leaders, a girl. "You didn't seem very with it today."

"Didn't seem very with it," Sam had learned, was a sly euphemism for "You didn't work at all and what you did do was awful, thanks for nothin'."

"Just got distracted today that's all, I think I just need a nap when I get back."

"Well, we're going to go to worship when we get back to base but if it's going to level out your brain then you better go take a quick nap."

I'll tell you what's going to level my brain out, those pills, those pills that are so neglected in my backpack. They'd balance me out for sure but I don't need them. I don't need them just as much as I need you and this worship time. I don't want one more 'holier than thou art' faux prophet with a six string telling me how to love something that I don't know I love anymore, so there. You can have your worship night, I'll just get back in my bed, maybe I'll look through everyone's jeans and hope I can find enough money to hop me a bus right the hell out of this torn down spit hole while you go and "worship."

"Ok, thank you." The true response had availed; the other answer slouched back down in its chair soon after, forgetting it had ever even been an option. Back at the base when he tried to lay his head down, he found out that he could not. A swirl of disruption swept over him and he could close his eyes. He began to think of how much he wished he had both taken his medicine and how much he wished he didn't have to. This dreadful symbiosis he now had with medicine was something that Sam was in an abusive relationship with. He was not even sure if he was in need of them anymore. Whether this was true or not, he didn't know yet. Since the introduction to the drug Ritalin in the 7th grade, he had been put on several different medications for a few other mental issues such as ADHD, depression and appetite loss, and an odd muscle tic that he had developed as a coexisting result. This wasn't painful, but he would randomly twitch his neck, blink his eyes together, or feel the impulsive need to pull his eyebrows out all for sensory stimulation, a sort of ADHD hedonism. Sam's gregarious nature was becoming more hyperactive and turning people off. He did not find many people who could stay around him for very long. Overall he was an uneven mixture of idyllic and psychotic. Nobody seemed to understand him, not even Sam. When he felt out of place he tried to do something for positive attention and feedback; a sort of affirmation that he was still good enough. That night while he was in the dorm alone, his mind knew just how he would get it.

It came suddenly, like a little tiny person with both a halo and a pitchfork on his shoulder. It wasn't a person though; he knew full well it was his medicine talking to him, making him someone who could rationalize his irrational behaviors. He called the man Will. Will was a combination of the three drugs he was currently on; Starterra, Wellburtrin, and Xanax. Sam struck up a conversation with him. Truthfully, he was getting really sick and tired of talking to things that weren't really there and wished his mind would choose between fantasy and reality and stick with one already.

"What are you doing here?" Sam started.

"You're all alone," observed Will.

"I just need to be alone."

"No, you need to be among friends."

"How would you know?"

"I know best, I'm what's best for you." There was a paternal comfort in the man's voice that was softly trusting.

"I'm better off without you."

"I'm not entirely sure you are."

"What makes you say that?"

"Look around you."

"There's nothing here."

I'm here Sam, don't listen to him.

Sam glanced, swearing he saw something on the opposite shoulder, someone else out of the corner of his eye, but there was no one.

"Exactly, you're all alone."

"I don't think I am."

"You are!" Will was very harsh, saying this—almost as if he was forcibly trying to convince Sam of his further deepening solitude.

"Why didn't you take me today, huh? Why did you abandon me?"

"I didn't abandon you, I forgot you."

"You remembered, but you wanted to see how you could function without me. You couldn't do it, could you?"

"No." Sam wanted to say yes, but he knew better. Will knew better.

"Because I'm the oil, Sam. You're the machine and I'm the oil, the new battery. I keep you running properly and when you don't charge your battery, Sam, you start to lose power, just like you're losing power right now."

"I'm fine."

"Fine!? Sam, you're sitting alone in a room talking to yourself."

The illusion broke for a fraction of a second and Sam surveyed his situation. Will was right; there was nobody else around, not even him.

"Battery doesn't seem to need recharging to me."

"That's because you haven't seen yourself without medicine, no, not yet. But I can show you that side of you if you'd like. It's very ugly, and everybody will hate you even mo…"

"People do not hate me. They just…"

"They just what? Can't stand you, right?"

"They have issues with handling me. I am not hated. I am loveable and capable."

"You are tolerated and limited! You can do nothing without me!"

"I can do all things through Christ who strengthens me," he said, firmly.

"Yes Sam, yes, I'm right here, reach out your hand, I can still grab you but you're slipping, falling fast, almost."

"You have no Christ, you have a crutch! That crutch is me, you lean on me everyday. When you have me, you are normal and when you don't have me in you you're a wreck, you're a mess, and you are unmanageable to everyone around you, including your own self, and now that you've made me mad I'm going to do the same to you Sam, make you mad!"

Sam blinked at the shapeless thing on his shoulder, this Will, this peculiar little entity.

"Who *are* you?"

"I'm whatever you want me to be: a friend, or an enemy. If you are a friend to me then you'll take me, taste me and let my round little capsule dissolve in your mouth and I'll work on rewiring you so you can be around everyone else like a normal kid. You can be just like *everyone else*, Sam. However, if you are an enemy, than I have no choice but to show you what an enemy I can be, I'll have to make you put your hands over your eyes because a thousand rooms will feel like they're closing in on you. A thousand rooms with a thousand more noises all playing at once. The truth is, without me Sam, you just can't be good enough. Isn't that what you want? To be good enough?"

Sam took in the believable lie and thought good and hard on it. If he took his pills, Will would be winning and that is something that Sam did not want. If he didn't take them, Will would be losing which was something that he did want, that was something that was good but at what cost, his tarnished clarity perhaps? No, he wanted to win…

And he had promised himself he would, someday… but when he had no cards left to play and push came to shove, he wanted to be accepted. He took the three capsules in their containers, shook them out into his hand and took them all at once. It was not a suicide attempt, it was a sanity attempt;

however the mixing of an ADHD drug, an anti-depressant, and a pill for anxiety attacks were not supposed to be popped like candy, a mistake Sam was about to find out he had made. When a group of six or so of the kids from the team walked into the "living" room across the hall from the dorm they saw two things: a pillow, and a wide-eyed Sam Reed holding it and muttering to himself. One of the girls immediately rushed over to him.

"Sam! Sam! What happened!?"

"I did it, I did what he told me to do...took the pills, took 'em all, all those little fuckers are inside of me, they ain't goin' nowhere now."

"Sam did you overdose on something?"

"Took my meds."

"How many pills did you take?"

Sam avoided the question and instead swallowed a wad of spit to moisten his dry throat.

"I'm really thirsty." He said.

Sam got up and walked towards the sink, grabbing himself a glass of semi-cold water and chugging it down fast.

"Sam...did you just try and kill yourself."

Brief pause for thought.

"Yes." he turned his face down.

Lie.

"Why, Sam?" The girl, Kylie, came closer to him and placed her hand on his shaking body. Sam looked up, consumed in her concerning sincerity.

Sam had not tried to kill *HIM*self; he had tried to kill something that he thought was a part of him and in doing so had put his actual body within harm's path. Sam had died in order to live, *or had he lived in order to die?* He knew he had lied to them as soon as it came out but somehow, it made him feel better. It was the togetherness, no, it was…what the hell was this?

Sam knew it as attention but a strange new kind that lacked mocking and degradation. It was sympathy. It felt good, it felt…overdue. It killed him to take advantage of it but being as he was not in his right mind, he did so anyway. Sam was under the influence of the effect of a clash of medicine.

"Sam, do you want us to pray for you?"

"No." *Why did I just say that? Of course I do, 'bout the only thing that can save a crippled soul like mine these days.*

"I'm going to pray for you anyway, I know you need it right now." This was so urbanely said, the epitome of that good old Lynville friendliness that Sam couldn't help but appreciate her religious vigor. Hers was bona fide and it was a nice heave of relief to see. Not many people would have said such a thing and meant it, so he let her in, and he let God come in as well, thanking him for unfailing Christian perseverance; it was what he needed though it was not something he wanted.

The rest of the group gathered around Sam who was pale and shaking, oiled with a light coat of perspiration and placed their hands on him. The prayer was a good one and he felt they had all rehearsed their lines well. "Dear Jesus" *or, you know whoever still cares about me enough to listen.* "We pray for Sam, that the beast won't be able to enter his heart anymore." *You kidding me? He's got his own throw rug set up already, Damn, I don't even know it yet and here I am rambling on about how cozy he gets in here sometimes.*

"Can I ask you a question?" Sam piped up.

"Absolutely Sam, what is it?"

"Does God still love me?"

"Why wouldn't he?"

"Because of what a wreck I am."

If the Sam five years ago had heard this he would have had a heart attack. *Wreck?! Wreeeck!?!? Sam, you ain't seen wreck yet! You've got a few cannon holes in you but your ship's not sinking yet, just you wait, buddy. You'll know what wreck is soon enough.*

The girl dove deep into her immature puddle of faith to yank out all that she knew of this subject.

"God's love is unconditional, Sam. I know it seems like such a simple concept but it can be hard to understand at times. It is not a love based on who we are, where we have come from or what we have done in our past. It's a love that stays constant, even when we don't want it, deserve it, or even know about it. It doesn't waiver, change, or end. Even though you think you might be at your worst Sam, God's love is going to remain true."

Sam just absorbed this and nodded his head. Being as he was still off his rocker a bit, fragments of what he had just heard implanted themselves and remained.

"You're going to be alright, Sam, do you want us to go and get one of the leaders for you?"

"No, I'll be fine; I just need to go back to bed."

"Ok, well if you need anything God is here and so are we."

"Thanks," he smiled half-assed and excused himself from the room, wanting to be alone.

It was quite possible the most perplexing and bittersweet feeling that Sam had yet experienced. This was Sam's mad world and though he had just lied about killing himself, he hadn't. Justifying his actions, he tried to tell himself that he had been trying to kill something that was inside of him, that dammed Will fellow. He had, but Sam, while just very high right now and in sort of a drug-induced nirvana, would be perfectly fine by morning.

Somewhat perfectly fine.

There would be changes coming to Sam from this point

on in life that he would not have ever seen in his wildest and most troubled imaginations. Sam was about to undergo a stunningly depredating metamorphosis to emerge unrecognizable as something he never knew he was going to become. It was going to be a half and half creation of those two beings from the beginning; the one everybody wanted him to be, and the thing he feared the most: a bad metamorphosis, but again a necessary one because without this change, Sam could not hope to see the light that he so longed for. As far as Will, or the hellhound, heck, as far as Lee Renwick was concerned (that stinkin' dead varmint) Sam had only just begun life. He was seventeen years old and about to enter his (first) senior year of high school, one that would fly by and be forgotten just like all the others. He had gotten over one of two speed bumps he would face. The first had been one of fear; he had conquered a representation of what he had feared the most which had been being alone. This second one would be a little trickier. The speed bump of self-realization...of coming to terms with the person he was supposed to be. Again, fighting with the two people he was and finding which one he was going to hold on to.

Sam actually went to the dorm and got himself into the top bunk in the corner like he said he would, but he did not go to sleep. Instead he stared mindlessly at the ceiling, wondering and waiting for a sign that something bigger was ahead of him. Bigger than lying to people and certainly much bigger than listening to strange men who weren't on his shoulder.

"Where are you, God!?" frustrated and running out of patience for this guy who was supposed to be there at all times but for whatever reason...wasn't.

"Unconditional," he thought. "Bullshit...he can't even talk to me." Sam needed an audible voice that would grow hands and shake him. Anything subtle and he would be convinced that God wasn't listening. Sam felt like even though God had saved his skin a few times before, he had done so out of habit and that his compassion and love for someone like Sam grew thin. This made Sam feel even more like a burden, and he hated that.

Believe it or not, the hardest part of Sam's life was yet to come.

Part III:
Metamorphosis & God Sobriety

Metamorphosis: (n.) a marked change in appearance, character, condition, or function.

"Who are you?" said the Caterpillar.
This was not an encouraging opening for a conversation.
Alice replied rather shyly, "I-I hardly know Sir, just at present- at least I know who I was when I woke up this morning but I think I must have changed several times since then."
"What do you mean by that?" said the Caterpillar sternly.
"Explain yourself!"
I can't explain myself, I'm afraid Sir, said Alice, "because I'm not myself you see."

    -Lewis Carroll, *"Alice's Adventures in Wonderland"*

...But the essential intention is the real sin. A man who cannot choose ceases to be a man.

    -Anthony Burgess, *"A Clockwork Orange"*

I do not understand what I do. For what I want to do I do not do, but what I hate, I do...for I have the desire to do what is good, but I cannot carry it out.
For what I do is not the good I want to do; no,
But the evil I do not want to do- this I keep doing.

    -Romans 7:15-19 *(NIV)*

I remember thinking,
Maybe I will come back
When I'm ready.
But I won't tell the other children
what it is like.
I'll have to make something up.

    -Richard Garcia, from the poem "Why *I left the Church"*

There is not a righteous man on Earth who does what is right and never sins.

    -Ecclesiastes 7:20 (NIV)

Hello darkness, my old friend.
I've come to talk to you again.

    -Simon & Garfunkel, *The Sound of Silence*

August 2005: Fall

7:34 am.

No Rain.

Sam had slept little that night and eagerly anticipated that morning's private devotionals that took place on the beach below. Disregarding his Bible, all he grabbed was his notebook and his trusty pencil.

That was the real handgun.

His words were the bullets.

He loaded it up and shot, and shot, and repeatedly shot, pumping that notebook's guts full of as much lead as he could.

Then, in the middle of a sentence, paused, clouded with thought.

Certainly in the grand scheme of life what had happened the night before was nothing more than just some extra added acting experience. Sam had in no way meant to mislead anyone with such a stunt, but for character's sake would and could not bring his mind to admit to himself, let alone anybody else, that he had once again lied about something terribly serious. He beat his brain raw wondering how on earth anyone could possibly be this compulsively deceitful. The reasons were many but the logistics were not there. Did he do this out of a need for attention? If so, there had to be better ways of securing attention than flat out lying to people, to their faces, especially about what he had lied about; killing himself.

Sam would not make the connection for about five more years that this compulsive need to lie was in fact related to his ADHD, which needed constant stimulation. In order to keep his physical hyperactivity under control, Sam's brain had to work double time to find ways for him to be stimulated, and one way the brain found this stimulation was through lying. It was wrong, of course, and Sam meant no harm when he did it, and in fact most of the time he was unaware that he was even doing it, but it was exciting. Maybe not to him but to his brain, and it drove it, fed it, so much so that it had turned it into a habit. All of this caused Sam's head to ache terribly and since, in his mind anyhow, the situation wanted to be dead already. He allowed it to do so and he moved on, putting his head back to where it should have been…in Mexico and the real reason for his being there.

But he couldn't fix it. It was still broken.

It provoked him, not an awful amount, but just enough to avert his focus. As the sun continued its ascent over the Pacific, a pod of dolphins lightheartedly made their way across the water and Sam appreciated them from the distance of the shore. They were bringing him joy; they were the sun in the storm, but the storm was still there.

The lies were the haze and the haze was the lies.

There was nothing he could do to fix it, was what one part of him told the other, but the other part of the body said to go tell the truth immediately and get the venom out of your system. Sam did neither; he just sat there on the sand, indifferent, taking no sides in the matter. Perhaps if he did nothing then he would feel no guilt, which was, of course, a lie, and he knew it but he did not want to know he knew it, so he ignored it.

He looked around briefly at everyone who was done with their journaling and getting into small groups for prayer. Sam just sat there trying to avoid the eyes of everyone else, just for now at least. He distracted himself with something else that had been bugging him for a while now. Before Sam and his team had arrived in Tijuana they had gone through training for what to expect down in Mexico at a base in Los Angeles. Every morning and night they had a worship gathering. One was optional, the other mandatory. Sam had never gone to the optional one and stayed inside of the room where he had set up camp and just read his Bible, going over certain verses and writing poetry as well if it came to him. He felt that was a much more productive and spiritually beneficial use of his time rather than being crowded in a room full of people and being expected to become instantly "intimate" with God. The worship leader there was not one Sam had taken any liking to and at one point, during a mandatory worship night in the middle of a song that Sam was just beginning to get into, (He did not normally do well worshipping in front of a crowd of people but he had let his hair down for Jesus.) all instruments stopped and the leader, rabid with what seemed to be a misplaced sense of what true worship was, shouted in to the microphone "I *want everyone in the room to stand up and raise their hands. Everybody should be raising their hands; everyone should be on fire for God right now!*"

Looking around, it seemed to Sam that everyone else had been forced to be on a similar level because people began standing up and raising their hands as they sang. He had given it absolutely no credit at the time but the thought had been festering inside of him and it was no mystery as to why. He simply did not understand why the guy felt he needed everyone to do this. *Did I miss something?* He thought to himself as he stared around, befuddled.

Wasn't the raising of the hands a sign of surrender to God, not to man? It came off to Sam as though the man was forcing everybody to worship, something Sam didn't think that was right. There could be no doubt Sam connected with God most through worship. Being lost in the music and experiencing it as though it was allowing him to rise right up to heaven was the greatest feeling for him.

He remembered the first time it had happened to him, last year. It had been at a worship night at another church. In the middle of a song he felt as though his body had been possessed by the music, his hands were high in the air, his feet were dancing, and he was not just singing he was…feeling the words of the song as well. But this time that feeling had been disrupted, offended…and questioned. It was the first time he ever really felt "turned off" by a person of faith. It was an instance that did not taint his own beliefs in the least so he let the idea fly away from his head when it was ready to and continued in his writing. He didn't revert back to the night before, he didn't want to.

After the morning devotionals, everyone made their way back to the base for breakfast. Sam got a bowl of cereal and joined some of his group members who asked if he was doing better. He said he was and this was true, he really was. All he felt at the moment was conflict within himself, nothing really more than that. In order to shy away from the majority of the conversation he put an extra helping of food on his plate and ate at a particularly slow rate. Afterwards, he felt a little sick and went back to the bathroom to wash his face, which made him feel better. He looked at himself in the mirror and for the first time really noticed that he looked nothing like the other boys. He just stared at himself and how unimpressive his body was, but it seemed as though there wasn't a whole lot he could do about it (which was completely untrue— Sam just lacked to motivation *to do* anything about it). He shrugged it off and went to the top bed.

Why can't I for once just not worry about everybody else and just focus in me?

This thought was the last of a stream of thoughts that made its way through the estuaries of wires in his head. Having the body that those other boys had was the last thing he thought about. Sam wasn't aware he had just entertained the strongest thought he would ever think.

After a few more weeks of ministry in Tijuana, Lynville, Washington was called home again. The trip had truly been the eye opening experience that he had expected but had not shown him what he thought he was going to see. He had seen a side of the faith he followed that had turned him off. He had seen that he was still in line for being the center of all the problems the world had to offer. Even so, he would face them without the assistance of his pills. He would never go back on medication again.

Inside he was becoming more and more apprehensive towards his religion but once again, his oblivious nature struck him full, and he did not know that Christianity was turning him off more and more. The fire he had once felt so passionately was slowly being poisoned by a toxic logic he had not yet come to realize, but soon would. Signs of his spiritual collapse were already showing. The lying was getting worse, the poetry was getting darker, and his lust for men was bordering on an insuppressible level. As dark as this sounded, Sam continued to go about life with a religious vigor that kept him distracted from the demons he was so obviously plagued by. At school, he was steadily making more friends and didn't put up with a whole lot of harassment. He hadn't officially "come out" but most everyone knew about him and nobody really bothered him about it besides the occasional idiot hick or jock. They had been cleverly clumped into the same category being as they were both equally vexing on his nerves.

The core group of friends that Sam had accumulated was steadfast and for the most part he got along with them splendidly. He found belonging—with those who belonged nowhere else.

Looking at them as a group one might consider them to be somewhat of an island of misfit punks. There was a Hispanic girl, Natalie, who was mostly into music that nobody had ever heard of and kept to herself for the most part. Her family had just moved up from the ghetto part of Houston and she was fairly shy. She didn't know very many people here, and most of them thought she was weird. One might say she was a closeted lazy genius with extreme potential but got made fun of so she kept her brains in her head and did not let them slip from her mouth. She was the tough one, the smart one, and the modest girl who made exceptions and was by no means reserved.

Later, after they both graduated, Natalie and Sam would often be mistaken for a married couple for the way they were always seen together bickering and laughing. Quite simply, they were inseparable. They told each other everything and shared the fact that they were both basket cases. Though they would have their fights and disputes, both knew it was improbable to live without the other and so they would always work past their troubles. Though Natalie never really talked about her past, it had been a rough one and Sam rarely brought it up. He accepted her silence at times for a sense of reminiscing of happier days and knew she had her issues just as much as he did.

A few other girls that had not been blessed with the popularity or features that all the girls in the 'popular' crowd had, joined into the group as well. Of all the outcasts, the queen and undisputed leader of the group was Candie Hilton. Describing her physically was not necessary and made no difference. It was her unchangeable attitude and bombshell personality that was by far the most incredible aspect about her for there was nothing like it. At best, she was simply this: a pirate and a gangster trapped in a British man's body that had been part of a punk band in the early to mid 1980's. The lovechild of Marilyn Monroe and Sid Vicious. That was Candie, a radiant rebel and a radical rock star wherever she chose to walk. Someone you would see on a highway asking you if you were "going her way" with a seductive and at first seemingly desperate undertone. If you said you weren't she gave you a right old "fuck off" looking the other way without even blinking, like she would be able to make it on her own no matter where she was going. Candie was a full figured girl but had an impeccable taste in fashion nonetheless, though it was certainly not a conventional one. Her light blue jean jacket covered a "The Clash" shirt and was covered in a song lyric. "The Aquabats" was in giant lettering on the back along with an anarchy symbol with safety pins and buttons everywhere. There were runs in her black leggings which met her black skirt at the upper thigh. She wore many necklaces and there was a ring on almost every finger. The makeup on her face was dark and dramatic but nothing compared to her hair. The indecision on color and length changed about every other week. Right now it was a dark chestnut brown and came down just past her ears. At times he wondered if she used Alexander McQueen as inspiration or if it was the other way around.

The first time Sam met Candie had been two years ago at an end of the year event for middle school. Everybody in 7th and 8th grade had been taken to a waterslide park. He had been chasing Candie and a group of her friends around one of the outside pools. Taking one great leap out of the water, he forgot that he had not tied his swim trunks together and off they slipped. He was standing in front of the entire pool butt naked with Candie and the rest of the group laughing their asses off. Sam and Candie had been inseparable best friends since then.

The entire group put up with the same amount of bullshit from the rest of the school, but was as thick as thieves and never left each other's side no matter what. Right up until they reached graduation. For Sam, even though he had stayed an extra year, still felt as though it had all flown by. Sam had finally made the break out of his shell and had attended all of the home football games with his other classmates. They were mates now, he liked them, and most of them liked him back. He had gone out to join the swim team and had run track as well, improving himself in both. Now the question he was faced with was what he was going to do with himself. He was anticipating a relaxing summer sabbatical but threats by his mother had proved to him that hasty employment was necessary.

With the final chapter of school written, so was the final chapter of life with his church. Sam was stunned to find out the senior pastor (the same one that had guided him through his profession of faith) and youth leader at his church were retiring. Not only that, but all the friends he'd grown up with had graduated and were moving on with their lives. Sam couldn't grasp the reality that all of these familiar people in his life were now abandoning him. Not purposefully of course, but in his eyes the friendships and such that he had worked so hard on forming now felt in vain and once again he was being left all alone on the playground. Upon returning to church when the fall quarter arrived, it was not the same for Sam. Nothing was. Lost in an unfamiliar void he found a new connection at another church. Settling in with new friends, Sam hoped to recreate the comfort zone he had once had. Though Sam was encouraged for a while, church life became stagnant, but he made the best of it. He enjoyed going to a special worship night that his church put on every Monday and he usually sat in the very back writing poetry about both his living love and dying love for God. He joined in passionately on the songs he liked but mostly kept to the back and worshipped in his own special way.

The post high group at his church had invited him to give them a try; so he did and by so doing met someone who knew he was looking for a job.

"Pam's the one you want to talk to. Just tell her I sent you and you should get it."

"What would I be doing?"

"You'd be working with the kids. Do you like kids?"

"Yea, love them."

"Then you should do just fine!"

The next Sunday after service was over, Sam sought out Pam and told her of the girl who had referred him.

"Do you have any experience working with kids?"

"Yes, some, I assisted with Sunday school at my old church. I read the Bible for my senior project." All of this was unfalteringly true. For Sam's senior project in high school, he had wanted to write a book but had not known that doing so in seven months was practically impossible and also did not know the amount of work that would go in to such a project, he just knew he wanted to write a book and had sat down one day presuming to do this. It was not until a meeting with the mother of a dear friend of his had told him that maybe he was jumping the gun on this one and needed to slow down.

"Maybe in order to write the greatest book, you need to read the greatest book," was the advice she had given him, and perhaps it was true. Sam was so eager to become a master that he had spent little time being a "student." So, in four months' time he did just this. He was the student, learning all that he could learn from the Bible both as a writer and as a Christian. Every Sunday, he would come into his friend's mom's Sunday school class and present what he had gathered from a book of the Bible that he had read that week to a group of fifth graders—something that he found both enthusiastically fun and mentally taxing at the same time but he loved every second of it.

"Do you go to church now?"

"Yes, this one." *True.*

"How many services do you attend a month."

"All of them." *Not true, maybe two a month.*

"Do you drink alcohol?"

"Sometimes, up in Canada, with friends."

"Ok, that probably needs to stop."

Sam at this point was not one to question authority but this puzzled him.

"I can't have a drink with my friends?"

"Well, I mean, if one of the kids saw you…"

"Whoa whoa, whoa. If one of the *kids* sees me in a bar then *I'm* in trouble?! Because if one of those kids sees me drinking at a bar then I'm not entirely sure that I'm the one you should be talking to."

"Sam, I know it sounds silly, but it's just a rule. Can you be okay with it and obey it?"

Sam was certainly not in the habit of drinking often and when he did he never got drunk…

I'm not like that one guy you see, what's his name? I can't remember, don't matter anyhow. I don't drink to dull the decay, I ain't no drunken man. That's it. That's the sonuva gun's name, I remember now because the name fits him so damn well, like a glove that's been worn so much but can't be brought to the garbage because there's so much fear in letting it go.

…nonetheless, it was something he enjoyed doing and

figured that what she didn't know wouldn't hurt her and said that yes, he would stop.

"Ok, well that's about all I need to know. All that I need you to do now is fill out this application. Even though we're already going to hire you, it's just standard."

Sam received the two stapled pages and looked it over. It was the basic information that would be found on any application but being as it was for a church the questions dove deeper than just "how did you hear about this job" and "what are any special skills you have that you feel qualify you for the position you're applying for." Stuff like that. There was one question asking if he'd ever been convicted of child molestation and then the familiar "do you drink" question.

We've been through this before, I don't drink unless you drive me to drink, got it?

Sam didn't feel like he had anything to worry about.

"What is your sexual orientation?"

"Damn. Of course *you're* on here, I knew *something* was missing from the checklist."

He thought long and hard on this, scratching his head, then his balls, then his knees which decided to become nervous as well. More time may have been spent in the question's deliberation that the filling out of the entire application. In the end, honesty prevailed over employment and he hesitantly wrote "homosexual," figuring they weren't going to take him but at least he was going to feel like he wasn't hiding anything. Something Sam didn't feel he could live with very well. He finished and reluctantly handed the papers back to the woman in charge of his fate. She scrutinized the entire application with a laser-eyed precision but said nothing about the answer he had put for the box marked "sexual orientation." She looked up and cast an amiable smile at Sam.

"Can you start this Sunday? That's going to be

tomorrow actually."

"Sure," Sam said returning her indulging smile.

"Wonderful, meet me here at 8:30 tomorrow morning and I'll let you know what you're going to be doing."

And with that, they shook hands, and Sam made his way home. It really was just that simple. He would start working at his church the next day.

♦ ♦ ♦

September 2008: Self-Mutiny

It was dreary and raining when he woke up to the gray sky hanging dead above him on that Sunday morning of his first day at work. His mom had already left for church somewhere else. A hot cup of coffee was sitting on the kitchen table along with two eggs and a few strips of bacon. It was a boring sort of morning but for some reason those were always the best. He figured people would feel as uninteresting as he did and so it was.

His job was easy, as he quickly found out. All he did was drive out to a sister church and assist with the lesson there. When the kids came in the classroom, he would greet them and do crafts and such. It was something that came naturally to him and he tried to make as fun as possible and with the group of kids that he was working with this was not hard at all. Standing up against the wall, he smiled at them all as they passed through the door (he could not wait until he had kids of his own. Then, glancing over his shoulder, he saw a pair of dark brown penetrating eyes.

Standing up against the wall, Andy Starr was a typical tall, dark, and handsome. He was dressed in a camouflage hunting jacket and a tattered hat he wore for a trucking company. Andy was also surrounded by a crowd of girls.

Sam couldn't stop drooling. Suddenly he noticed Andy noticing him, and quickly turned his gaze back to greeting the kids; mortified.

In the middle of telling one of the children what sort of craft they were supposed to be working on he felt a shadow behind him and looked up to see who it was. It was Andy, but he didn't know his name yet.

"Hi…." Sam had his classic blank stare expression. He had snapped himself out of the dreamy glaze.

"Andy." He extended his hand, towards Sam.

"Sam, nice to meet you." Andy shook like a man; firm and serious but with a childlike smile on his face that made Sam feel like world hunger had just been solved.

"I'm sorry if I'm interrupting you while you work but I thought I would come over and introduce myself." Sam looked over where the crowd of girls had once been and found that they had all dispersed into the sanctuary.

"It's alright; it's very nice to meet you Andy." Sam's tone suggested that he was budding into a hopeless romantic and he didn't even know it yet.

"I haven't seen you around here before, did you just start attending?"

"I've been attending this church but at a different location. This is my first week working here though."

"That's excellent. Listen, I was wondering if you would like to grab coffee sometime."

"Coffee? Umm, sure, I'd love to."

"When is a good time for you?"

"Umm, well I have a lot going on today; I'm usually not free until the evening."

"Well then how about tonight?"

Sam wheezed unexpectedly and tried to hide his shock with an awkward smile. He was kind of famous for those.

"To-to-tonight?!" Was this actually happening?

"Yea, tonight!"

"Ummm...well I'd have to..." Sam thought about asking his mom but trashed the idea. "Sure, I'd love to," he finally said.

"Sounds good, man. I'll pick you up around 9 then."

"I'll...see you then." His response was slow; he didn't believe he was actually going to be hanging out with Andy.

The truck was parked right outside by the bus stop just like Andy had said, so Sam had no difficulty spotting it. He fixed his hair one last time before opening the door and seeing Andy there with a smile on his face. The two said hello to each other and from then on they spent the better part of the car ride getting to know each other. Andy was a man's man. He liked hunting, fishing, trucks, sports, everything a man could possibly like. He operated a semi truck for a hay company and almost never slipped out of his tan, stained Carhartt jacket. Despite his clothes, however, he was very built and clean cut. He kept hair gelled and facial hair trimmed. Curiously enough he never brought up the subject of women, which Sam thought was odd, but perhaps something that Andy just didn't have the time for so he dismissed it. The ride lasted about a half an hour and they had arrived at Andy's house. It was a spacious place out in the middle of nowhere, but it suited him just fine. They got out of the truck and made their way inside. Sam went in first so he couldn't have possibly noticed that Andy had been checking him out the whole way up the stairs. As he entered the house, Andy told Sam to never mind the clothes on the floor and to just make himself at home. The place wasn't a terrible mess but it was evident that Andy wasn't a clean freak. There were bottles of alcohol across the counter and dirty dishes were visible in the kitchen. Andy shut the door behind him and told Sam to just throw his jacket wherever he wanted to, locking the door and closing the blinds well before turning to face Sam.

"Do you smoke?" Andy asked as he pulled a tattered carton of cigarettes and a lighter out of his jacket's left side pocket. He lit the cigarette and let it smolder in his delicate spit-stained lips.

Although Sam actually despised the reek of cigarettes, he wanted to show Andy that he had that sort of rebel side to him, that he did have the capacity to be somewhat cool and not just some nerdy wannabe fag. This wasn't just some other guy, this was Andy Starr, and Sam needed to be at the top of his game. He wanted to make a good impression on Andy so he could have the chance of being invited back sometime. Even though he thought Andy wasn't gay, he still felt the unrelenting need to impress him. He hesitated before finding what he deemed to be a decent response.

"Yeah man, I smoke like…four cigarettes a day." A suitable lie he thought Andy might buy.

"Wow, a whole four, you must be on your way to some crazy emphysema at that rate!" Andy said this in a very sarcastic manner and Sam knew he must have said something stupid so he attempted to redeem himself.

"Well, that's on a not so stressful day, on a regular day I can smoke as much as eight." After this, Sam considered picking a different topic to lie about next time.

"Well either you're a terrible liar or a terrible smoker. Andy chuckled as he said this and Sam smiled tensely. Andy looked at him and said somewhat solemnly, "You know if you don't smoke you can just say so, it's really not a big deal." Sam knew this but didn't say so.

"Well, the truth is," Sam started, "I-I-I've never really done anything before." Sam could feel the embarrassment make its way out with the words right as he said them and turned his famous shade of red, totally concerned that Andy was going to take him for an even bigger loser than he already was if that was even possible.

"Anything? What do you mean by anything?"

"Well," Sam started, "stuff like smoking, and drinking, and...well, I mean, I've had drinks in Canada but..."

"Ever had sex?" There was a tamed charisma in Andy's tone when he asked this and it propelled Sam's stagnant sexual drive further to unfamiliar ground.

Sam was well caught off guard by this question, which came out very casually as it would by a guy like Andy. Once again Sam was at that point of wanting to seem cool, but also not wanting to be found out a liar this time he responsibly said... "No, I haven't." but, before Andy could interject, he slipped in a "not yet anyway, it's not like I don't want to I just...haven't yet." Sam's attraction for Andy was steadily rising, as was his hopelessness of ever being with him. He thought he knew the kind of person Andy was and the kind of people he hung out with and a kiss, let alone anything more than that was out of the question. Sam could only sit on that couch and look at him with a growing lust and desire and do nothing about it.

Andy looked right back at Sam, sort of inhaling him; surveying him over. Maybe it was out of Sam's innocence or his sincerity, or perhaps he just found him to be a little bit pathetic, whatever the reason, Andy smiled at him with one of those guilty smiles that made you would wonder if he wrecked your car or slept with your best friend.

"Would you like to...

Kiss me?

...Join me in a drink?"

"Ummm...sure, what are we drinking?"

"A personal favorite of mine, screwdriver."

"Alcohol? I, I don't think I can drink tonight, I mean if I go home and my mom even thinks I've been drinking she'll kill me for sure."

Sam was painfully nervous at this point. This was all very new to him, not only that but he felt uneasy about something else that he couldn't put his finger on it. Some sort of illusive fear that had buried itself somewhere deep inside his subconscious and was knocking on the door wanting to get out but unable to do so.

"Do you need to be home at a certain time before mommy calls the police wondering where you are?" Andy chuckled while he said this. "You know you can crash here tonight if you'd like, it's no trouble."

"Oh," Sam said, agreeably surprised and secretly excited about the offer. "Do you have an extra bedroom?"

Andy grinned, not normally but somewhat...Sam was looking for the word to describe the look in Andy's eyes when he asked him this and it almost seemed as if the right word would be...devilish, a devilish intent of a grin.

"You can sleep in my bed, how about that?"

Sam just about wet himself at these words and it must have showed how shocked he was because Andy laughed and told him to close his mouth and put his eyes back in their sockets. Sam expressed his amusement than apologized.

"You know something Sam, I've known since I first saw you."

"What's that?" Sam knew exactly what he was talking about, but he wanted to beat around the bush and evade it as long as possible but he knew it wouldn't be avoidable forever. And so it wasn't.

"That you're gay."

Uh-oh, Sam thought, *busted!* Quick, start talking about something straight, umm, football, titties, car parts, cows, anything; pick a category! Then he paused and thought for a second.

"Wait, if you know then why are you being so cool about it?"

"Why wouldn't I be?" Andy replied knowing where Sam was probably going with this and fully prepared for it.

"Well," Sam started, "I mean you haven't beaten me up and you even invited me to spend the night in your bed. I mean, what straight guy would ask that?"

Andy smiled, no he grinned, as if he had expected this. "What makes you so certain I'm straight?"

There was that lifeless silence again before Sam began to stutter out…

"…I-I-I know you are! You have to be, I mean you're always with those girls at church and they're always…"

"You ever see me kiss any of those girls? Ever hear of me dating any of those girls?" Everything was spoken rather brusquely as if he were trying to get Sam to spit something out faster because Andy already had in mind what he was going to do.

"Well…no but I-I just assumed…" Sam wanted to be dumbfounded but he didn't have time to be. Andy came out of the kitchen with the drinks and extended Sam's to him. Sam took it, still absorbing everything that he was hearing.

"Thanks." Sam looked at Andy with a naïve charm. He didn't know what else to do or say and in order to ease the tension, mentioned that he had never drank before. He said it felt as though it was somewhat of a taboo thing to be doing, especially with Sam being a minor and all.

"Not at all," Andy said as he grabbed his drink and took a sip and joined Sam on the couch, "it's just alcohol. Trust me, this isn't the first or last time you'll drink so don't savor it or anything, just go for it, ya know? Grab life by the balls. Truth be told, I didn't want to go to church that day but I'm glad I did because I got to see you. I thought you were pretty fucking cute." Andy spoke this with a certain authenticity, which turned Sam on without him even knowing it. Actually Sam had never been turned on before so the feeling was a first and he enjoyed it.

"You really surprise me, Andy."

"Why's that, stud?" he smiled at Sam

"I didn't pin you for the…well, my kind or anything like that."

"Well I can't exactly go around announcing it to everybody, can I? I'm guessing you can probably share that feeling. If anybody at the church ever found out about this little get together of ours, I'm sure neither one of us would have our job there for much longer would we?" He winked at Sam who didn't know he was blushing.

"Yeah, I guess I can." Sam just continued to mindlessly ogle him.

With only a faint smile on his face, Andy placed his hand on Sam's thigh. He had looked as if he might have wavered in doing so at first, the look he had let Sam know that he was, beyond a doubt, confident of everything he was about to do.

Then for some reason, everything just stopped.

Not showing that he was lost in thought, Sam's mind created the most vivid of images and thoughts. Through the courtesy of years of religious oppression and cultural sheltering, Sam had yet to even learn what sex really was. He had heard of how heterosexual intercourse was supposed to work, but hell if anyone talked about how to go at it with another man. Yet right there in that moment, as inexperienced as he was as to what he was about to say, let alone do, he knew that this "new magic" that was happening right in front of him, was right. The right-est form of right there was and then, in that instant, looking into Andy's eyes, he made a choice. Maybe he made it without even realizing it; no that was untrue, he knew full well he made it; he wanted to make it. It was the pivotal moment that would be a defining role in the years to come. The actions he was about to commit himself could not have, in that moment, revealed both the pain and pleasure they would later cause him. He did not see that, he couldn't have. For the time he was doing what any kid his age would've done, and that was anything that felt good, and this first guy, this first time, was definitely going to feel a little more than good.

The space on the couch between the two men grew narrower as they inched closer to the more intimate company of one another. Hesitating only briefly, Andy began to massage Sam's leg moving it up and down, caressing down to his kneecap and sliding it back up to his upper thigh where his budding erection enthused. Sam could barely understand Andy when he told him not to be nervous although it would have had little effect on him and his increasing heart rate. Both of their eyes willingly met and magnetized. Inches away from uniting lip and tongue, their hot breath collided in the middle and without even realizing it was already happening…they had kissed.

It was only a kiss…

Seeming to waste no time their arms were corralling one another as their bodies tried to be as close to each other as they possibly could. The sound of lapping tongues was insufferably erotic. Andy's hands had made their way up Sam's back and Sam's hands were running through Andy's prickly-gelled hair, making it smooth again. Their lips had unlocked briefly and now all they had was the enticing draw of each other's eyes. Andy drew away momentarily and looked at Sam, both of their breathing already very heavy.

"Well, how does it feel so far?"

"It's amazing, I'm really enjoying this." Were the words Sam said and it was the truth, he could think of no other thing in the world that could feel more right than what he was feeling at that moment, and whether it was the utter sense of finally being able to break free from the shackles and chains that were his golden boy reputation, or his raging boner prominently protruding in his pants, something compelled him to go further and he had no desire to ignore this impulse.

Before he pressed his mouth towards Andy's again his faith *did* come to his mind for a minute or two, realizing in this instant that he was going against every bit of conscience that was telling him he wasn't supposed to be doing this. *Supposed to.* The words were now unpleasant tastes in his mouth as though he had just dry swallowed a bulky capsule full of bitter medicine. What had compelled him to believe in this credo for as long as he had? How had he sat through those religious ceremonies for so long? For so many years he had allowed this deity to regulate his life. He had been a faithful servant and steward, and now there was this part of him that wasn't certain if his heart had ever fully been in this to begin with. Faith is a funny thing we all have inside of us. Sometimes we know it's there, without a doubt, for God; other times, it can be placed. In Sam's case, he had been adhering firm loyalty and trusting devotion to a deity, uncertain if that same devotion was being given back to him. Sure, there had been Mission trips, small groups, Sunday school, and Bible study and they had always managed to be at the top of Sam's list. He never gave a second thought to what else might be out in the world. He had seen himself as almost impenetrable to the "sins" that the world had to offer. He always thought that he was going to be protected; thought that he would never succumb to any of them. Sam simply thought that he was too good for temptation. But now he was discovering that none of these things protected him from sin, and for some reason, he was very thankful for this.

Time to get back to reality.

"I'm enjoying this too," said Andy, returning Sam's attention to the couch, to the drink, and to the man he was with. "But it's a little cramped on the couch here, how about we go somewhere where we have a little more room to spread ourselves out."

"Sure, ok, sounds good to me." Sam's tension and nervousness were slowly seeping out of not only his voice but the rest of his body as well and he was becoming more and more comfortable with this proud, newfound sense of self-mutiny. Andy grabbed Sam's hand and escorted him down the hall to the bedroom. Before entering Andy turned around to face Sam and they smiled at each other and then kissed, they kissed their way into the bedroom and onto the bed where Andy got on top of Sam and put his hands under his shirt, removing it at a somewhat slow pace. Lips still locked, both of them removed the other's clothes with fervent desire. Andy removed Sam's pants finally freeing Sam's caged erection. Andy instantly grabbed it in his hand and began eagerly stroking making Sam moan in pleasure. Sam took off Andy's t-shirt and ran his hands over his chest, twisting his nipples a little and then running his fingers down his rigidly level abs. Andy unbuckled his own pants and Sam slid them off, looking in awe at Andy's tumescent cock. He slowly savored the task until at last they were stripped, exposed, and unprotected. All that was left between them was nothing but primal, lustful intention.

"I want you, Sam."

"I want you too Andy." If the words hadn't been spoken they easily could have conveyed the same message with greater intensity with their eyes. Both knew what they wanted, and both were going to get it.

"Come here," Andy whispered.

Sam wasn't nervous, he knew he should have been but he could not explain the ease he felt in that moment. He trusted Andy, and was ready to do whatever he was about to do. The two men wrapped up each other in the other's arms once more except this time, there were no annoying pauses for thought, and they didn't let go.

The next morning Sam awoke figuring what had taken place the night before was just a fantastic dream but when he realized he was in an unfamiliar bed and Andy was still asleep next to him the sweet reality had set in that it had in fact, happened. He yawned and looked out of the window to find that the sun was not out as he had expected it, but in fact it was raining quite hard. In Sam's head however, the sun was out. It was shining brighter than it ever had and nothing was going to extinguish the happiness he felt inside. He rolled over and kissed Andy on the neck and a few seconds later Andy began to stir, turned to his side and opened his eyes.

"Mornin' stud," said Andy still groggy but smiling.

"Hey there. How'd you sleep?"

"Hahahaha, well, after I got done with you, I gotta say I slept like a baby."

"Is that a bad thing?" Sam wondered out loud.

"No it's not bad, it means you tired me out..." And after seeing Sam's continued expression of uncertainty he ended with "means you were good, silly!"

Sam smiled, relieved, after hearing the flattering accolade. His inner self made a little downward elbow thrust with a "Yes!" in a sort of hissing sound. It was pleasing to know that he had done a good job. Being able to make Andy happy made him happy.

"And uh, how did I do if I may ask?" Andy grinned as if he already knew that the answer was going to be a positive one full of praise.

"I gotta hand it to ya, Andy; you're a star from bicep to butt cheek."

Andy let out a satisfied belly laugh in appreciation, and looked at Sam for a few seconds, once again, surveying him.

"How has a stud like you never been with anyone, huh?"

"I don't picture myself as much of a stud, just a kid."

"Well you certainly don't screw like a kid."

Sam soaked this in; he certainly wasn't doing a whole lot of things like a kid anymore, was he?

"What time is it?" Sam said suddenly.

Andy told him that it was about 8:45 which means Sam was already late for work and needed to get going. He went into Andy's bathroom and doused himself in deodorant and cologne since he had no time for a shower and hoped that would be good enough. Both of them threw on presentable clothes and made their way out of the house, down the stairs, into Andy's semi and made their way to the church.

When they got there, they both decided that it would be for the best if they did not walk in together as the pastor knew of both of them being gay but was unaware they knew each other. Sam went in first and entered the room where the kids were already doing pre-lesson crafts and playing with each other. His boss came up to him almost immediately inquiring where he had been and why he smelled like he just stepped out of a Calvin Klein ad. He apologized for both his tardiness and his aroma and began his work. During the entire lesson, he couldn't stop thinking about last night and about Andy and the actions that had left him feeling nothing short of superior. From that point on, life began to move at an even faster pace for Sam. In the next month he tried to further his relationship with Andy without knowing that he was going to get himself into one heck of a predicament.

There are certain kinds of people in this world that are known as "deceivers" and those who are not deceivers are called "receivers." Those known as deceivers (Andy) go around and make everyone believe one thing when in fact what they want is for the receivers to be distracted by their deception. The receivers (like Sam) hear and believe everything that they are told by the deceivers because up to this point they have been hurt so badly by others that they hold onto anyone whom they believe "loves them." Sam was in love. Andy had cruel intentions, and, to him, Sam's heart was just something to be chewed up and spat out again. As usual, Sam was blissfully unaware of all of this and he always continued to see the best in everyone—a trait that was fuel for a man like Andy.

During this time, Sam had once again found a sort of silver lining in the chaos, which had helped him cope with the heartbreak. Sam had formed a friendship with a girl he had met at a youth retreat some years earlier and had been able to pursue a more in depth friendship with her.

At a petit 5'2", Jenny Cline was nothing short of a personality firecracker. Her outward appearance channeled her Christian upbringing but with a mixed influence of The Ramones and Shaggy from Scooby Doo. Jenny and Sam shared a similar taste in music and both of them knew how to party, something that Jenny was introducing Sam to at fast rate. Though neither of them knew it at the time, they were both in similar places with life. Jenny was struggling with her faith just as much as Sam was. It would be safe to say that they were both straying from the path of goodness. Jenny had her faith, but at the moment it was on the back burner while she explored other aspects of life. Sam had already done this and did not see himself as 'lost' or 'strayed' but simply beginning a new chapter. This was not to say that Sam had completely abandoned all morals and principles. Assuming something like this would be untrue. Sam simply didn't associate himself with the Christian faith like he used to, Jenny was different, she would eventually return to the God she loved, but until that point came, she was determined to live her life, and bring Sam along for the same ride.

Thus far, the only interaction Sam had with drugs at this point was with his medication which in retrospect had done much more harm than good to his brain. The mixture of more drugs might have had worse consequences than foreseen. As it was, Sam would never get into the heavy drugs that Jenny would, but nonetheless that wasn't what was important. You see, to someone like Sam, it wasn't the doing of such drugs that would have an impact on him, it was more the exposure, being around something he had never been around before, not to mention something that his upbringing had taught him was wrong. It gave Sam that inflated sense of superiority that he had never gotten in school; being able to do what the 'big kids' were doing. It made him feel a part of something. It made him feel cool, like he was good enough to fit in with of these people even though none of them really gave a shit who he was. Sam would finally feel that he belonged and no one would judge him.

None of this had happened yet. In fact, Sam had yet to meet any of these people or experience the things he was going to experience. He had barely even started smoking, which was a big enough deal to him let alone his mother when she found out, but on one particular evening this would all change. He was sitting in his room when he got a text from Jenny saying that she and a couple of other people were going to a party and wanted to know if he was down to kick it. Sam replied that he was game to hang out and about ten minutes later Jenny arrived at his house.

"Where going?" said his mother who did not look up from her book but knew Sam had the intention of not being home tonight.

"Out with Jenny, not exactly sure where," was the vague answer he provided.

"Are you staying the night anywhere?"

"Not that I'm aware of, mom, I'll call if that changes."

"Ok well just leave a message because I'll be going to bed here within the hour."

"Alright." And with that, Sam kissed his mom on the head and went out the door where Jenny was waiting for him. She was in her teal Ford Taurus that they had affectionately named "Sugarlips" after a name off of a fruit box Sam had gotten from a grocery store.

"What's goin' on, dude?" said Jenny as she smiled at Sam. She looked cute tonight in her 'Pink Ladies' jacket, black eyeliner, and converse. Jenny was a child of the 90's and her clothing style announced this daily.

"Not much man, what's the game plan for tonight?"

"Dude, we're going to this rad party at my friend Ian's house."

"Sweet, what are we doin' there?"

"Gonna…*party it up!*" Jenny had this thing that she did where she would sometime end her sentences in a high pitched voice and Sam always laughed at this. Jenny told Sam to pick out a CD and he chose the ever wonderful Pat Benatar and they rocked out to that for a while. Sam and Jenny made small talk but didn't really dive into anything serious until about halfway through the car ride. Sam instigated the conversation.

"Jenns, what do you think we're going to be like in a year?"

Jenny didn't seem shocked by this question, but possibly was taken a little bit off guard.

"We're still gonna be *best fuckin' friends forever

139

dude." She did her voice thing again. Sam laughed.

He took it as a sign that this wasn't really something Jenny wanted to talk about at the moment and he didn't want to bust her high so they kept driving and laughing and singing. They were at their destination before they knew it. Jenny locked the car behind them and they walked the gravel pathway from behind the alley to the front door, knocked, and were greeted by Ian.

Jenny jumped in to the introductions.

"Ian, this is Sam, he's my best friend, Sam this is Ian, he's super cool."

"Nice to meet you," they said simultaneously and shook hands.

Ian invited them both to come on inside and make themselves at home. The place was a little on the empty side in the manner of people but Ian said that they were expecting many more to show and to just hang out. Sam sat down on the couch where Ian's female pit bull Marilyn had also decided to seat herself. Now, Sam had never been attacked by the pit bull, but nonetheless he had his reasons for thoroughly disliking them and therefore moved. Jenny came back from the kitchen and to Sam's surprise held a beer in her hand. Sam did not know that Jenny drank, and this was not her first time doing so.

"Dude, I didn't know you drank?!"

"Hell yes! It's awesome," and before Sam could even respond to that she asked him, "Do you want me to get you one too?"

Immediately, Sam knew two things: how he wanted to respond and how he *should* respond. The voice in his head; the crumbling conservative voice, piped up briefly at first, coaxing him to engage in no such debauchery, though this voice was faded and made no impacting reverberations. Sam decided it would be permissible, if just for this one time, to blend in with everyone else and have a little beer already.

Up until this point in life he had drank illegally once, at Andy's, right before…

"Yeah Jenns," he said calmly but not smoothly.

Jenny handed him a bottle which he looked over carefully.

"Thanks babe," he told her with a smile, and Jenny took a seat beside him and began engaging in conversation with a couple of girls that were across the room from them.

Sam continued to survey the beverage that was in his hand. At first he was reluctant to smell it but he did anyway. It was a difficult scent to describe and certainly not like anything Sam had ever encountered. It had the crispness of a pine forest and the antiquity of an old leather jacket. He took a sip. It was bitter, so a cringe came over his face. He looked around and was glad no one saw him. A girl who obviously did not have a dislike for beer came semi-stumbling in from the kitchen to announce that they would be making a beer run so that a game of beer pong could get going. Sam turned to Jenny and asked her what the hell beer pong was.

"Dude, it's this rad game that you have to play!"

"Ok, what do I do?"

Jenny explained that you and a teammate are given two ping pong balls and six red plastic cups. They would be in front of you in the shape of a triangle, and the same amount of cups in the same shape would be set down on the other side of the table in front of the other team. All cups would be filled a quarter of the way with beer. The object of the game was to take the ping pong balls and try to throw them into the opposing team's cups. If you made it in then one of the team members had to drink. The object of the game was to make the opposing team drink all of their beer before you did. Sam said this sounded simple enough.

He continued to hold his first still-full beer in his hand, nervous that people would notice. The party scene was something that was brand new to him and he had no idea how may beers he should've chugged by now. Something that you have to understand about Sam is that he has been, and most likely always will be, not like everyone else. He was not yet as mentally developed as the rest of the kids his age, so although most of them had been drinking beer since about sixteen, it was something that Sam still considered to be somewhat of a taboo subject. He had grown up around a mother who had not only been left by an alcoholic husband, but had explained that alcohol was something he needed to stay away from, that he should never ever drink it and up until this point had not been shown otherwise. Alcohol to him was something that was "bad." To the normal brain, this would have been immediately disregarded but to Sam it was something that was taken to heart and he really did feel guilty about what he was doing. However, determined to still have that part of him fit in with everyone else, he did not let his nerves show. He erased the look on his face and drank the rest of the beer with a heavy heart. He got a glass of water as soon as he was finished. It was not long before the rest of the crowd came back from the beer run and began setting everything up for the game.

"Sam, I need you to do me a favor." Jenny turned to him with a serious look on her face. "I need you to drink for me."

If Sam's nerves hadn't shown before, they were pulsating throughout his entire body now.

"Why do you need me to do that?"

"I have to drive dude, and if my parents find out I've been drinking they're going to kill me."

"And my mom is going to be thrilled?"

"She's going to be asleep when you get home right?"

"Yea, but still…" The battle was already lost, though. Sam was the kind of person who would throw himself under the bus for his friends and though he knew he was being used by Jenny on one level or another, he just loved her to death and didn't want to see her get into trouble. He said that he would drink for her.

They all gathered around the table, started the game and not even two beers into the game, Sam started to feel it, and he still had four beers left to drink. There wasn't a gratuitous amount in each cup but it was a lot for someone who wasn't on the same binge drinking level as everyone else in the room. The room wasn't spinning but Sam could definitely feel that his mind wasn't moving as fast as he wanted it to; it was taking him longer to react to situations. There was little doubt that he was getting drunk and it was happening very fast and even though he was winning the game in front of him, he was rapidly losing his sobriety.

"Jenns, I odnt tihnk I cn drisnk anmore man." he tried to gather his words but his brain didn't care, he was too gone.

"Dude, you're almost done, just one more drink Sam!"

Sam drank, but afterwards fell with a thud to the ground. That damn light was growing thin again, and he was making his way into a new darkness.

He blacked out for what seemed like a minute or two and when he regained consciousness he found himself in Jenny's car, still drunk, and going in and out of the world. His eyes were glazed over like a dead deer's eyes after getting hit by a truck. He could hear Jenny trying to make herself known to him and her words were entering his ears, but not his brain.

"Saaaaam, yoooo gaahhhhtuuhh waayyyyk uuuhhhp maaaaan..." His head was rotating back and forth like a screw coming loose from a rotten floorboard. The windows were rolled down and he could feel the cool night air groping his face and his hair. It was not raining and the efforts did not shake him awake enough. He could not be shaken, he was elsewhere. Sam was north of the rain and south of the darkness. Where did that leave him? Hawaii? He didn't know. He didn't know anything right now. Darkness…conscience…darkness…conscience. It was battle that his mind and body could not choose a side for; he just swayed and bobbled like a bottle lost at sea. No, he wasn't the bottle, he was inside the bottle; he was inside what was inside the bottle.

"You gotta wake up Sam!"

He regained semi-consciousness long enough to know what she was trying to tell him. Jenny was going through a drive-thru at a McDonald's in order to get Sam some food, something he should have had long before he began drinking. All the Big Macs that place had weren't going to make the drunkenness disappear. In fact, eating one would most likely induce more vomiting but then one way or another it would be helping him. Jenny's speech was fuzzy as she spoke to the automated machine for she was a little bit sloshed herself.

As soon as they got the food, Jenny ripped open then bag and almost tossed the burger into Sam's mouth which he chewed, half-assed, before swallowing. He washed it down with the large diet coke.

Still in the darkness. Couldn't see a thing, couldn't do shit about it.

"Come on buddy, you gotta wake up."

Truthfully, Jenny was panicking more for her than for Sam. If they were to be seen by a cop and found out that both were under the influence and underage then it was curtains for them. Finally, Sam mustered up just enough energy to keep his eyes open the rest of the fifteen minute ride home. Jenny tried to ask him questions in order to keep him awake but his coherency was not salvageable so she kept driving and rubbing his shoulder to keep him from passing out again. Sounds continued to go in and out; he could hear the music leaking through the stereos.

"But it's just the price I pay, destiny is calling me. Open up my eager eyes..."

Something was calling him, the hound? No, this wasn't his field.

"Open my eyes, open them up, please, I need to use them." He was talking to himself again. It was an entity of wonder and cataclysmic glory, a being of divine omnipotence. He could taste it, almost. He opened his eyes, as eager as they were to be closed and saw...nothing. Not a spec, not a god, not a star. Jenny once again woke him from the drunken daze.

"Can you make it in alright, buddy?" They had arrived at Sam's house.

"I tinkn soman," he slurred his speech, talking aimlessly as he stumbled out of the car. As soon as Sam was out of the car, Jenny took herself and her car and drove home where the consequences of her own actions were waiting.

As she slept, Juliet was awakened with a bang coming in through the door and up the stairs. She didn't bolt upright for she knew it was her son, but something was wrong. She got up and headed for the door but stopped short to listen. Juliet recognized the unsteady stair climb and the reckless dive for the commode. The murmuring, muttering, and mumbling of the Drunken Man was a shattered song she had heard before...once by a husband, now by her son. As the sounds continued from the bathroom and she heard the hurling, she lowered herself back into her bed. She was afraid, knowing he was home safe but she still worried. Dark, tainted memories came seeping back to her mind. She remembered the nights when Drunken Man would come tumbling in through the door and into their room, the back alley bar whiskey still fresh and hot on his breath. He would slide into bed, clothes dangling from him, and his tongue would slither out of his mouth trying to touch her neck but she would refuse him. He would slur about how much he loved her and she would close her eyes tight and tell him to leave her alone. He would make his way to the couch. Come morning, they would marinate in an awkward silence while Sam just took the invisible bullets that they fired back and forth at each other with their eyes.

Juliet continued to listen, the tears slowly leaking out. Was this fate that had destroyed her marriage now invading her son? Even though Sam did not have an alcohol problem and had simply made one bad decision, to Juliet, one bad decision like that could lead to many more. The familiar fears were closing in again and Juliet held on to her faith, although she felt that this could be bad decision number one of many more to come. She listened.

Sam stumbled into his room and for a minute or two made no noise.

"Maybe he's not drunk, maybe I'm just overreacting." She hoped this hard.

Sam threw up again, it was all over his wall and in his bed. He was too drunk to clean it up and blacked out.

Juliet knew it was real. Sam knew it was real as well.

Waking up the next morning, Sam was close to knowing two things: the first being that he had a tremendous headache and he felt like a pile of bricks was on top of his him, holding him down to his bed. He had a hangover. The second thing he knew was that he was in serious trouble. His mother had already left for work but there were three objects on his bedroom floor. A bucket, a sponge, and a note which was sitting inside of the bucket.

'We'll talk later.'

Was all it said, there was no 'have a good day' or 'love mom' anywhere on it and Sam knew he had stepped it in big time. He looked at the crusted vomit on the wall, chunks of cheeseburger were still hanging on but mostly that ghastly alien goldenrod had plastered itself everywhere. He was finally able to get up. He grabbed the bucket and cleaned up the mess in both his room and the bathroom. Jenny texted him shortly afterward, asking if he was alright. Sam said that everything was fine and when she asked him if he wanted to hang out tonight he said yes. Truth was, he didn't want to be home. He couldn't look his mother in the eye and tell her he got drunk even though both of them knew he had been.

"Fuck," he sighed out heavily.

Hanging out with Jenny from then on proved to only get worse. It was more getting drunk, more late nights without a clue where they were, and more meeting people he never wanted to meet again. At this point Sam was certainly not coming because he wanted to, he just felt obligated to be there for Jenny's sake so that he could keep an eye on her. He was a Jiminy Cricket to her more than anything. He had held his tongue for as long as he could but every time Jenny had come up to him with that drunken smile on her face, and for every bong she put her lips around, Sam was finding that holding his tongue wasn't going to work for to happen much longer.

A few nights before Jenny and Sam would have their blowout, the both of them along with Candie and Natalie went to go see a new 'friend' of Jenny's. His name was Johnny Buckley but Jenny and the rest of his stoned out crew affectionately called him 'Uncle Johnny.' But not Sam. He had qualms with him as soon as they met. Johnny's long scraggly hair was greasy and parted unevenly down the middle. His breath reeked of popcorn through his canola oil yellow teeth and Sam could smell it from across the room. When he walked he had an obvious limp but did not use a cane or anything to assist him with walking. Hearing him speak was just an unpleasant as looking at him. He boasted no book smarts aside from his unlimited knowledge of weed and sell out rock bands from the 1970's which were the peevish basis of his conversation. The apartment he lived in was a trashed out hole in a run down apartment building for disabled people. Beer cans and issues of Rolling Stone Magazine were scattered around, some in piles, others hidden under newspapers or on top of dressers. A glass table with knick knacks was at the center of the living room which had an array of dead plants and a tank of fish in the corner. The fish must have taken after their brain-dead owners because their house too was a mess. There was a see-through curtain with the Grateful Dead logo on it that covered the open window. It was very chilly outside but for 'ventilation' purposes they had to keep it open.

Natalie, who had taken a similar dislike to Uncle Johnny, had ostracized herself on the couch next to Sam while Candie sat in a nearby chair next to Jenny. Uncle Johnny was in the chair furthest from Sam and he was happy about that. Sam and Natalie just sat in the corner avoiding everything. An ambulance went by and the sirens startled many people in the room who mistook it for a cop. Sam and Natalie sort of laughed at this. They had nothing to hide.

The night dragged on for what seemed like an eternity, but they had really only been there for about an hour. To Sam, and Natalie it was an hour far too long. Jenny sat in the corner with Candie who was packing some weed into the small glass pipe and lighting it up. There were many captivating sounds to smoking weed which Sam was in denial about because he didn't want to bring himself to say that he enjoyed this at all. The click of the lighter, the fire hitting the hash and sizzling it all downward as the inhale, exhale, sigh of relief followed. It was all so poetic to him. It was like a ritualistic dance and this made him curious. He just continued to watch, sort of transfixed and disgusted simultaneously. Sam watched and watched and would've kept watching if Jenny hadn't broken his concentration.

"Sam…do want to try some?" she mouthed to him across the room. Natalie was texting someone and not paying attention. Sam thought about the question for a little bit and considered both the nonchalant air in which it was asked and its impact. Now, if we know anything about Sam at this point, it is that he is not only very desperate to fit in (not exactly in this situation, he could have cared less for these losers, but he wanted to prove to himself that he could actually do it), but also that he is a very curious individual. So at times he falls victim to the sinister pranks of his curiosity. This would be one such fall where Sam's curiosity, despite his want to protect Jenny, would get the best of him.

"Can I smoke it in the bathroom? I just don't want Natalie to..." He was going to say that he didn't want Natalie to see him smoking because he felt like she would be disappointed in him and he didn't like it when she was upset with him. She had the tendency to make sure Sam never forgot anything he did (good or bad) but Jenny understood where he was going.

"Yea, that's fine dude."

"Umm...how do I, do this exactly?"

"Just hold the pipe by the base and keep your thumb by the hole on the side right here, when you light up, suck in, take your thumb off the hole and suck in again. Hold it for as long as you can and then exhale, got it?"

"Yea, I got it."

"Let me know what happens," Jenny said with a proud smile on her face.

Sam excused himself and told Natalie he had to go to the bathroom.

"Ok," she said without even looking up from her phone.

Sam took the pipe and the lighter, went into the bathroom, shut the door behind him and locked it.

He stared at it for a little bit; it was a curious twisted and colorful piece of green and blue glass and smack dab in the middle of the hole, the good stuff. He smelled it. It was a new smell, nothing he had ever smelled before could compare to it. It was like an evergreen tree in a compost pile that had the lingering smell of a skunk on it. It was an enticing scent and not repulsive in the least even with the slight skunk smell. He took the pipe and held it as he had been instructed, clicked the lighter and a tiny yellow flame rose from its metal mouth. He touched it to the bowl and watched as the sparks danced on top of it. He inhaled too much the first time and coughed heavily. It tasted like herbal popcorn. Now he knew why Johnny's breath smelled that way. Sam drank some water and caught his breath and lit up again. The second time he tried it, he inhaled and kept it inside as long as he could until he began to feel fuzzy then let everything out.

As soon as the drug hit his brain, something radiant happened and it happened with a tranquility very alien to Sam.

He dug for a pen in his jean pockets and felt one, fiddled with it, attempting to free it from its awkward position. He noticed a roll of toilet paper that was sitting, purposelessly on its spool, double quilted and substituted his systematic college ruled for it. He wrote as he regularly did, without thinking, just the first words that came to his mind. He opened up their cell door. No, that wasn't right. He had given the drug the prison key. It had unlocked the cell door for him, and what a world it had unlocked. His mind spaced, went to space, needed some space to space his words, the words were in space and he had to go looking for them...he found them, somewhere between the drug's pleasing mind nirvana and the sixteen balloon-like moons of Jupiter, he found them. He sucked them in with the weed's smoke and let them out through the veins in his hands:

Casting iron on my hands, staring at gold before my very bright eyes
There's a cold brewing somewhere in my brain
I can't be in two places at once
If I get high now then shake your finger at me
Like a rattlesnake shakes his tail
Hiss hiss hiss hiss.
Poison, poison screaming voices
Pinned up on the wall like a dart board
Throw a hummingbird at my eye
He won't know what's going on
Neither will I. Everyone, behold my ultra-radiant omnipotence, everyone everyone everyone everyone!
I'm just lost on a cloud's sidewalk; get my soapbox in before it rains
A lizard who was pretending to be a rock turned to me and said "nice weather we're havin', eh?"
I told him to quit fakin' it
He turned back into a rock.
I felt bad for him. He's a little pathetic these days.
Line up and sit down at the table
I need you to feast on some metaphors
And other appetizing atrocities
But don't cut your hand on the tablecloth
It might excite the vultures.
I've told the butler not to take any more phone calls so come on inside
Have a cup of tea, relax, there's a rifle in the loveseat
It's mother of pearl, I tell you
Come lay with me in the big wheel.
We can have sex on the feathers of birds.
I keep them caged, they like to watch, they're naked too.

All of their feathers are on the bed in a pile, it'll be better for us
but perhaps you'd like

A drink before we proceed. Scotch? Maybe this funny clear liquid
should do the trick

It has the density of gasoline but I promise you it's tasty.

Promise…look into my bloodshot eyes and take another swig of
serenity. After that, it's

Lights out boy, there's a sinkhole of happiness under these sheets…

There was a series of harsh, loud knocks on the door but Sam, who had ascended from the bathroom and onto a euphoric sidewalk up in the sky, did not really hear it. He just paused before he continued to write more, he was in space, and there was no rain in space, just the lightning, bright vivid flashes of it. Sam could feel himself swaying, as if he were in a car that was recklessly changing lanes.

Changing lanes, changing lanes, we're changing lanes.

Back to what was going on. What the hell was going on? He was waiting, what was he waiting for? He was waiting for….

…Just a waiting for you and I, comatose eyes rolled over like waves
on the shores of Saturn

Sweeping the sky, taking me with them

I see the towering stairs in an unfamiliar home

Snow-covered steps, nothing is falling, nothing else is white

Foreign soldiers practice below, in the valley

Don't kick the rocks down, they have guns

I see his face, the most holy of smiles.

Perfect, Oh! Holy night, we embrace, then kiss

We are lasting, the joy is eternal
He the same, I, lost in this welcomed illusion
Pick up the money laying on the ground in Wonderland
Set it one your dresser in bundles
Catapult the flea and hear him yell
With all the other animals except for the turtle
He's fast asleep
Make your way through the wet, blue meadow
Come to
You're not there
He's not there, they aren't either
Smile anyway, at least you didn't see
The hound.

After he had written that, he surveyed it, not really sure what to make of it or of himself. He couldn't decipher a word of what it meant but he was high and he liked it so he stuffed it in his pocket and would decide what he would do with it later. Sam floated out of the bathroom along with a haze of clear smoke and waltzed his way over to where Jenny was.

"Dude, how was it."

"Fuckin' magical, man."

Jenny laughed at this. "Sweet!"

"Are we leaving soon?"

"Yea man, chill out, I'm like, almost ready to go." Jenny always said chill out, even if you were baked and she had no reason to be upset. Chill out was just her way of saying "soon."

Candie looked over at Sam and gestured to him if he had smoked and he motioned right back with his thumbs up, signaling that yes, in fact he had. Candie smiled and stuck out her tongue with a signature "wicked" following it.

"Sam, You're actually high!?" Candie said, surprised.

"Yea, I guess I am," Sam said, returning the surprise. He had just used a drug that hadn't been prescribed by a doctor. It was new territory and Sam liked it a lot, for now at least.

As elated as Sam was at the moment, there was little doubt that his patience with Jenny would grow even thinner once he stepped down from his irrepressible high. There would be more excuses about why she couldn't change or break away, why her 'friends' needed her around, and most of all, why she couldn't live without Sam.

The night came to an end, and as Sam began to float back down he realized what he had really done. It wasn't smoking weed that had bothered him. That had been incredible. It was the fact that he had encouraged it for Jenny. Sam was one of those people that Jenny looked up to whether she admitted it or not, and it kind of broke him a little to know that anytime she smoked from now on, the words "I don't like it when you do that" would have no effect because Sam had just done the exact same thing. In these situations of push and pull he turned on his music and was soothed off to somewhere else.

His church life was getting better and also getting worse at the same time. He felt more attached to the kids he taught and worked with every Sunday. The happenings with Andy couldn't keep a mystery for much longer. Either someone was going to find out or he was going to feel like everybody knew about it and just wasn't going to say anything. If that were the case, it wouldn't be long before Sam cracked under pressure. Worship was his romantic outlet towards God but other than that, sermons just went in one ear and out the other. Mainly Sam just focused on doing his job, and keeping his private life private, something that wasn't going to be private for much longer. On a particularly warm late Sunday morning after he had finished with work at church, his boss had come in saying that the pastor needed to see him about something. She said she didn't know what, but her look indicated otherwise. He made his way across the parking lot down to the offices to where his pastor was. The pastor was on the phone, so Sam waited outside the door until he was done. It wasn't long until he signaled Sam inside. He closed the door behind him and sat in the chair, looking the man in the eyes.

"Hello Sam. How are you doing today?"

"I'm alright. What's going on?" Sam tried to eradicate any and all signs of nervousness as fast as he could but was finding it a very tricky thing to do.

"Just checking in with you, that's all." His seriousness was subsiding and a relaxed, welcoming presence swept over Sam.

"Is there anything you want to talk about?"

"No." *Only that I like men.*

"You know you can talk to me if there is, right?" a stern paternal tone about him.

"Yea, I know that." Sam succeeded in keeping his cool, *but if I did that I'd be fired from this job and then I'd have to dislike you for a very long time.* "Well, there is…no."

"There's what?"

"No, it's nothing important." Sam said this in his "did I almost just give something away about me that will lose me this job and alter your personal evaluations about me as a person? I don't think I did" voice.

"Sam, you know that you can talk to me about anything, right?"

"Yea, I know." *I just don't want to. You wouldn't understand this one, preacher.*

"I just feel like there's something you want to tell me but you're nervous of what I might think."

Yep! That pretty much hits the nail on the head! Except if you knew what it was, you probably would never let me inside the walls of this extravagant religious institution for the rest of my days. Promise you that!

"Well, not nervous of what you might think per-say…"

No, exactly that.

"… I just don't want to lose my job."

"Something I would fire you over?"

Something that I wouldn't put past you to fire me over.

"Well…"

"Come on Sam, you can tell me."

"I…"

Both Sam and the pastor's impatience were becoming more and more visible with every avoidance of what Sam was trying not to say. Sam felt like there had been a ticking inside of his brain for the past few weeks and as much as he cupped his hands to his ears, it only got louder and more intolerable. That terrible feeling of being 'discovered' was surfacing, but he still felt like it was a salvageable situation.

"I've been drinking," was the slippery lie he clutched from the fish tank of stories swimming around rabidly in his head and ironically enough, it was very true. Sam had been drinking and it would be an easy fix as well. Alcohol was truly nothing he was addicted to and if he had told this to the pastor he would still be allowed to work as long as he went through some sort of minute counseling and promised to stop, but he did not say it. Instead he did what pained him most. He drove the stake in his heart and told the truth, and hoped sympathy and pity would be taken upon him. He crossed his fingers to the point of breaking them.

"I've been sleeping with someone." Sam felt a mass exodus of grief leave his body even though he had just killed his job without knowing it.

"Who?" the pastor oddly enough did not seem to be all that surprised.

A moment of brief silence and a drop of shame stained itself on Sam's t-shirt.

"A guy."

It was out. The toothpaste had left the tube and it couldn't be put back. Sam was slightly relieved and now his fate was in the hands of a man on a golden pedestal.

"Well, I appreciate your honesty, Sam…"

Thank you, because I totally could have told you it was a chick and you probably would have asked me if I enjoyed it. I would have said no, she tasted like a rotten tuna fish sandwich with warm mayonnaise. That's what they all say about it.

"…and had you told me otherwise I would have let you go and terminated your position here."

"Wait, you're not going to fire me?" Relief poured in by the buckets. Maybe there is hope for me and this man of God, maybe he's going to take the true Christian route and forgive me completely, giving me another chance because that's what you're supposed to do right? Right? Christians forgive. That's what they do.

"No, I'm going to fire you…"

Sam's hopes were immediately bulldozed over.

"…but I promise that you'll be leaving with a much clearer conscience now, won't you?"

A mental gasp of anger. Son of a bitch! You totally played me! You KNEW the whole time and you just let me sit and sweat bullets here in the heavenly hot seat!? The only thing I'll be leaving with is a new understanding of the people who claim to practice Christianity!

This was said wholly within Sam's mind, but the look on

his face said it all loud enough, mixed of course with a new sort of heartbreak.

"You knew?" Sam brought out the obvious just to see if it was really happening.

"I got off the phone with Andy's parents not long before I called you in here. The moment I saw you two talking at church a few weeks ago, I was afraid that something might be happening. His parents called me to tell me that he had told them what was going on, which confirmed what I had been worrying about. I thought that Andy had made the better decision when he told us that he was no longer engaging in that sort of unhealthy and unclean lifestyle but I guess once you fall, you never really get up unless you have the hands of Jesus to hold you."

Sam held back the vomit. As much as the majority of him actually kind of agreed with that last statement, it was hearing it from a man who, he felt, knew nothing of sin, and nothing of what God's love really was. He expected everyone to shake his hand and shout out hallelujah. The real Sam, plainly just didn't know how to react to Christianity anymore. One too many instances had shown him that there were more of these kinds of people who tolerated but did not love, showed concern but did not care, heard and read, but did not teach and learn.

What made him the most nauseous was knowing that he had not only let his church down, but his kids and the natural affinity he felt towards them was prying the back of his mind open like a large metaphorical crowbar.

They would have to be told that Sam wasn't working there anymore and even though he knew the reason for his leaving would only be talked about amongst his former employees, the sting was still there. The rain was there too.

This time, it was a downpour, and his body was being flooded by it; inundated with a newfound sense of understanding with a bitter dash betrayal. Even though Sam was still allowed to attend the church, he felt he would be under constant, heavy scrutiny and watched like a hawk. So though the courtesy was extended to him, he politely declined. Sam only attended a couple more services, after that, he never returned to this or any other church and his passion for Christianity slowly dwindled with every passing day. For Sam, the Christian faith just wasn't something he wanted to associate himself with anymore. Those people had pushed him out of their circle. So where did that leave him?

A day later Sam received a text from Andy saying he had to see him. The tone of the text was vacant and Sam thought something might not be right. Sam replied "ok" and twenty minutes later met up with Andy in the parking lot of his church.

"I can't see you anymore," began Andy, not hesitating or fumbling his words. Sam got the feeling that he had been planning this for quite some time.

"Why not?"

"Because I'm not gay."

"You sure didn't think that before."

"You were confusing me. I didn't know what I wanted."

"Oh, so I was your confusion?!"

"You were a disappointment and a mistake."

Sam didn't say anything.

"Life would have been easier without you." Andy had concluded his harsh statement with this.

"So where do we go from here?"

"I'm going home and I can't talk to you ever again." Sam noticed Andy said *can't*…not *wouldn't*, and tried to persuade this conversation towards a positive ending.

"We can still be friends. It doesn't need to end this way."

"It does. I need to live for God, not some temporary faggot boy toy. I'm a disappointment to my family because of this and I don't want that anymore."

"You don't know what you want. First you're gay in high school, then you're straight for a while, then after you've been fuckin' me for a month you decide you want to go on the straight and narrow. What the hell is your problem!?"

"You are!" Andy's voice was rising. "You know what Sam; I hope this life fails you. I really do. And when you finally realize what a fuck up you really are there's going to be no one to blame but yourself."

With that, Andy walked out of Sam's life. Sam and Andy would never see each other again.

Sam walked away too, unaware that he wasn't even crying. When Sam got home, he crawled into his bed and switched on the halogen lamp by his dresser and retrieved his pen and pad. The poem was as easy as a Bourbon Street prostitute. The voices in his words were understanding, angry, and loud. This first heartbreak was:

Excuse me, sir? What have you done?

Have you made me think this way just for fun?

I don't even feel like a consolation prize to your indecisive eyes.

Well bless your soul for thinking you had won the game, sunshine.

But that head you placed in the clouds

Got struck by your ego lightning one too many times

And scorched a romance already made out of dry eucalyptus

Funny thing is, I knew things of you…but they eluded me. Diluted me.

I watched you go back and forth between whom to love and

Whom you should love for.

But I refuse to compress this stress for you anymore.

It isn't worth it, not for this level of doubt

I tried to work something out

I was strong for a while, but I confess, not enough to resist the pressure of your smile.

Which hooked me like a persuasive, pervasive incantation

I sensed a foul error in our fornications

Unease in our mutual masturbations

You deceived a trusting heart

Believe me; I stood as much as I was able to do.

But I could sense second thoughts secreting themselves on the loveseat

That you staple gunned in the back of your blue and gray 16-wheeler.

There was talk of why you should not, could not, and possibly would not.

You said it was a sin that you gave in. I almost convinced you, it was love.

But the situation's salvation was lost.

And the tears I dropped were cancelled out by angel's praise

I heard that after you broke me in half that you were confused for a while

But that Jesus helped you find your spectacles

I guess heaven's chairmen decided to put out for you instead.

It really hurts to see you struggle and to notice you second guessing yourself.

But on the other hand, whatever choice you made of forgetting me was probably for the best.

I would have done it on my own eventually

To be briefly honest, I couldn't be prouder of you

I hope he gives you the happiness you never bothered discovering in me

And if you find me walking along the street with a stronger demeanor

Looking like I'm fine without you, my face out of the mud;

That just means I finally realized that you were the disaster

That satisfied me enough to want to be perfectly fine on my own.

Sam seemed to be losing a lot lately and he felt that's just what he was best at being. He was after all, still the playground's lonely, available loser. He went home, shut his eyes, and wished as hard as he could that he was a kid again. In the rain cloud he had made all by himself, wishing he would no longer have to be subject to the world and its mean, nasty bullies.

Sam was 19 when he put his faith on the back burner and decided to do things his way.

Sam was 19 when many things happened, apparently. He had tasted the flesh of another man. He had, with the same exact tongue, tasted alcohol, weed, and betrayed the one thing he had once loved so very, very deeply without question: his God.

Jenny continued to be there for him, and also furthered her drug use, her finagling, and her rebellion. She was now experimenting with speed, ecstasy and had briefly dabbled with cocaine. In many strange ways, she was on the same level as Sam. The two were changing together; they were going through a metamorphosis, wrapping themselves up in the debaucheries they were involved in to only emerge as better people and they were doing it together. Sam and Jenny had undoubtedly been through a lot already and their friendship was, as it would continue to be, on another level. How much they really needed each other though would be put to the test a few days after Sam's brush with old lady Mary Jane. Both of their worlds were about to crash, Jenny's especially. But for this to happen, in order for there to be light, there had to be the dark first.

And what a fantastical nightmare of darkness it would truly turn out to be.

Something was already different when a red Ford explorer pulled up fanatically into Sam's driveway. Sam had a terrible feeling that tonight wasn't going to be fun. Jenny told Sam that tonight was going to be great and to top it all off, Ruby was going to be there. Sam thought 'why not' and hopped in the back seat for the ride. Immediately after stepping in the vehicle, Sam could tell two things already. One, that Jenny was driving a car that was not hers, and, two, that she was already drunk. Ruby was sitting in the backseat, her seatbelt secured. He turned to her with anxiety already in the air before his words could make it out of him.

"Do you know what we're doing tonight?"

Ruby turned to him, rolling her eyes as she did so. "Apparently, we're going to these two guys' house and drinking."

"Ooh, how wonderfully original," Sam said.

"Ugh, I know right."

"I'm so sick of this, Ruby." Sam leaned in to say, "I've just…I've had enough." Ruby and Sam were making sure that their little tête-à-tête was kept in the backseat, but Jenny was out of it just enough to where she wouldn't have noticed anyway even if they had been talking normally.

"Have you talked to her about this at all?" Ruby, who had known Jenny even longer than Sam had, asked back, sharing an equal concern for what might happen to her.

"I think I've mentioned it to her, but I don't think I've ever offered any sort of ultimatum."

"Do you think you ever might?"

"Well, if this keeps up, I'm not going to have a choice am I? I mean, I'm definitely not looking forward to the day when I have to tell my best friend that I don't want to be around her anymore but I'm also not excited to see her picture in the obituaries section either."

"Exactly!" she said, her frustration mounting. "And I mean, there's only so much that we as friends can do and then we have to step up and be the parents; take away all of her toys and put her in the corner, you know?"

"Well, and I mean her parents don't even know what's going on or anything because she feels the need to lie to them so much. If they found out what was really going on then they'd flip shit for sure. Like, more than the usual parent. I know if my mom even knew I was going to a party, even if I wasn't drinking which I'm not, she'd still bite my head off."

"I don't know, man. All we can do right now is just try to be good influences on her and hope she snaps herself out of it."

Sam thought of the other night and what a terrible influence he had been on Jenny in front of all of those people, the people that he disliked the most. He wasn't sure if he could be the encouraging friend for much longer. Something inside of him had put up with enough and he was ready to snap. Subconsciously he was waiting for that one last straw to break his back.

The worn wheels of the Explorer scraped the gravel path of a driveway as they arrived. Jenny and her friend Jackie got out of the truck first while Ruby and Sam both looked at each other with a "let's do this" sense of unease. The night uncomfortably lingered surprisingly enough without too much drama. Basically everyone was just hanging out, drinking whiskey and beer, and eating pizza. Sam was doing karaoke which no one was paying any attention (he was extremely grateful for this) while Jenny was talking to Ruby over by the wall of the garage about what the both of them had done that day before meeting up. A young girl, Serena, one of those high school drop outs who was most likely pregnant underneath her brigade of sweatpants and in the middle of a drunken stupor, was wobbling past the two of them when she accidentally bumped in to Ruby. Sam sensed drama so he kept a watchful eye.

"Hey, wtch…whatcher doon."

"Sorry." Ruby paid her a glance and nothing more.

"No, M serrus, so much shits gun down tnight why u got start shit."

Sam concluded that her uneducated speech would probably not be different had she been sober.

"Well, it was totally an accident and I said I was sorry."

"Donbe sucha, why ya got'a be sucha bitch!"

Jenny stepped in, in a weak attempt to cool the fire but Serena pushed her aside and kept going at it with Ruby. Sam sat on the couch and to his own surprise was too enraged to do anything about it. If he stepped in, that girl's nose was getting broken. Sam was a highly capricious guy and had very poor impulse control due to his ADHD which continued to be hard to control. Sam's brain was unable to think ahead to possible consequences and could not conceptualize cause and effect. He would think about stepping in and punching Serena, but then people would yell at him for doing this, and he wouldn't understand why he was getting yelled at. Before he could even get up out of his chair, Jenny came over with the bottle of wine in her hand, irrevocably drunk—something that wasn't abating Sam's temper.

"Saaam! What's going on? Are you having fun?"

The statement's bullet made its way through Sam's chest and out of his spine, paralyzing and dumbfounding him with the audacity of what she had just said. He thought about what he *really* wanted to say.

"Am I having fun? I'm sitting on a couch surrounded by drop out,

tuned out, drunk ass wannabe has-beens with more past than future, whose lives consist of getting plastered, fractured, wasted, and stoned. I'm watching you down a bottle of wine while your best friend gets harassed and insulted by some overweight tattooed slut and this whole time all I can think of is how pathetic you've become and how much I don't want to be here. I want to be home! Away from these people, away from their lifestyle, and away from you!"

Sam wasn't thinking it anymore, he had said it out loud and Jenny had heard every single word of the tirade.

"What the hell…"

"I'm done."

"Sam, why don't you talk to me about this?"

"I have!! I have told you over and over that what you've been doing these past months has been destructive and irresponsible and all you can think about is you and what you can do next to fuck up your life. I'm not going to sit on the sidelines anymore while you trash yourself." The acrimony in his voice was rising with intensity.

"Sam, don't…"

"We're leaving."

"Do you hate me?"

"It's me or the drugs, Jenny."

"….I don.."

"Me or the drugs."

"Sam, you're my friend, and I love you man."

"Ok then. Prove it."

Most of what Sam had just said really didn't sink into Jenny because she viewed Sam as just one of those overly emotional people who tended to overreact in situations of high stress like this. Battling him when he was like this was useless and Jenny figured it probably was time to go before he got worse.

"Fine."

Jenny grabbed Ruby who had freed herself from the tyranny of the drunken bitch who had finally passed out on the couch where Sam had been sitting. He was hoping she would taste the anger that had been lingering there but she was too far gone, like he had once been too far gone. They piled into the truck. Jenny had gotten Ruby to drive her car home.

"I'm sorry, buddy."

Sam remained silent. Nothing else was spoken the entire car ride, not even a goodbye when he got out of the car to go home.

The emotional cut Jenny had made in the beginning of this toxic whirlwind had been gashed even deeper and this time, "I'm sorry, buddy" wasn't going to rebuild any of the damage that had been done.

◆ ◆ ◆

July 17, 2009

It was Sam's birthday. He was 21 years old. He had two drinks that day and no more. A group of his closest girlfriends had accompanied him to the movies to see the newest Harry Potter movie. Candie, Natalie, Ruby, and a few others were all there.

Jenny wasn't. They had not spoken to each other since the blowout a few days ago—Jenny out of shame, Sam out of anger.

After the movie was over, Sam and the rest of the group got out of the theater and as they were about to go the dinner, a familiar voice came up to the group and started talking to Ruby and Candie. He sensed the unwelcome presence of Jenny and sure enough it had been her. Sam played with his cell phone but was listening to everything that Jenny was saying.

In the front row of grabbing his attention was her saying that she lied about getting in a car accident in order to get money, which she had wisely spent as evidenced by her numerous bags of clothes and shoes. Jenny was more than adept to malingering and calling in sick just to smoke weed and drink cheap wine. What was more revolting to Sam was that she wasn't alone. Uncle Johnny and his group of inebriated fools flocked with him and Jenny like a thunderous train of error. As angry as he was at her, it wasn't having any sort of effect. Jenny was just refusing to admit that she was making some serious mistakes. Sam spat on the ground after all of this had sunk in. Jenny came up to him with her bags and attempted to be friendly, something Sam did not want to be.

"Happy Birthday, Sam."

"Thanks."

"Are you still mad at me?"

"Yes." He continued to look at her with a look that plainly said, *how could you?* and Jenny picked up on it right away.

Jenny looked down, then turned and walked back to Uncle Johnny.

That's all that was exchanged. No more. They all left for dinner shortly after.

A few weeks later, on a hot and lifeless night, Jenny was arrested due to a warrant for her arrest because she had failed to show up to court. She was sent to jail and shortly after went to a rehab in California, which of course Sam was powerless in. Having left things the way he did with Jenny had eaten away at him. What he had said to her had been two months or more of pent up frustration, angst, and hostile thoughts towards the crowd of people she had surrounded herself with. But Sam's feelings towards Jenny had remained unchanged. He still loved her, but she was over a thousand miles away at a rehab clinic thinking that her best friend hated her more than anything.

Truthfully, he was still mad at her for having been stubborn and learning the hard way. She had nonetheless most likely learned it by now and Sam wanted nothing more than his best friend back. He didn't hate Jenny and he knew he didn't. He loved her enough to let her go during a time when her hand couldn't be held. Sam knew if she was determined to do things her way then that's just what he had to let her do. He missed her drama and he missed her "spacey-ness" but most of all he missed his sister; his absolute other half. Without her, life sucked and the downward spiral that he had gone through with her was still imprinted on him in places. More promiscuity, more drinking, more flipping the finger to God and his screaming fan club. There was a recent bitterness about him that was utterly detestable. He didn't like it, but the other half of Sam loved it and two halves grappled with each other daily. Finding peace was not going to be easy, especially for this torn soul. It was going to take much more than a simple change to pull him out of his rut; it was going to take a full body revolution.

Part IV:
Revolution of a Renegade

Revolution: (*n*) a sudden, complete or marked change in something.

Yesterday, all my troubles seemed so far away,
Now it looks as though they're here to stay.
Oh I believe in yesterday.
Suddenly, I'm not half the man I used to be
There's a shadow hanging over me
Oh yesterday came suddenly.
   -**The Beatles** – *"Yesterday"*

Now I must rinse, she said. And this is how it rinses out.
-Stephen King, *"Misery"*

All the struggle
We thought was in vain
And all the mistakes
One life contained
They all finally start to go away
And now that we're here,
It's so far away
And I feel like I can face the day
I can forgive
And I'm not ashamed
To be the person that I am today
   -Staind *"So Far Away"*

Then you will know the truth, and the truth shall set you free.
   -John 8:32 (NIV)

Sam didn't see Jenny again for two months and during that gray time Sam didn't know what to do with the hole that his former best friend had left in with. He plugged himself into promiscuity and getting trashed try and fill the heart-shaped void. At least once a week, Sam was sleeping with somebody different. He didn't get tested, for any disease because he didn't care. Part of him wanted to contract something and let it run its course. Deep down though, he cared. Sam had well gotten over anything that Andy or anyone else had done to him at this point. He truly did want a meaningful relationship.

Part of him just wanted to let the hound get him, but he had seen nothing of the beast since his days as a hospital-bound invalid. In his hungry search for sex, he came across a man on the Internet, somebody not much older than him, who had sent him a message on Facebook one night.

Michael Kennington to you:

Hey. Nice profile, how are you?

That was all that were written. Sam clicked on his profile out of curiosity and saw that he was not only magnificently attractive, but that he also lived about 90 miles away from him.

Just my damn luck, Sam thought. The most beautiful man he had ever laid eyes on lived in a city two hours away and by the looks of it, the guy didn't drive. He knew there would be no chance of being with him, not for a long time at least but just for the hell of it, he accepted the friend request anyway. The chat window came up almost immediately.

MK: Hi! Thanks for the add!

SR: Hi there, you're welcome, have we met before?

MK: No, I just thought you were cute.

SR: *blush* aww thanks!

SR: So, what do you do with yourself?

MK: I'm a filmmaker. I shoot and edit videos for companies and friends.

SR: Is that something you enjoy?

MK: It's my dream job.

SR: Well, that's all that matters.

MK: What do you do?

SR: Recently unemployed.

MK: I'm sorry to hear that, are you looking for work?

SR: No, I'm going to take a break and figure out what I want to do with life. Might go back to school but I haven't decided yet.

MK: Well the most important thing is that you're doing something that you want to do.

SR: I agree.

MK: Well, I have to get to bed but I'd love to talk some more soon.

SR: As would I.

MK: Goodnight boi.

SR: Goodnight handsome.

Michael went offline and Sam was smitten in a way he had never been before. He knew he just had to meet Michael somehow but realistically the chances of that happening soon were slim to none. He just held his breath and hoped that fate was on his side. One month later, it would be.

During dinner one night with a new acquaintance, Thomas, a discussion of Thanksgiving had come up and Thomas had asked Sam what he was doing. Sam knew that his family would be having a dinner, but was not looking forward to it one bit. He lied and said he wasn't doing anything. Cordially, Thomas invited him to dinner in exchange for some help in the kitchen, which Sam certainly didn't object to. Without even thinking, Sam asked who all was going to be there and Thomas named off people he had never heard of until…"and also my friend Michael is going to be there. Do you know Michael Kennington? I think you guys are friends on Facebook or something."

Sam's heart blew up, reconstructed itself, and blew up again.

"Michael's gonna be there?" he said, somehow contorting his excitement into casual surprise.

"Yea."

"Oh…awesome!" He was almost speechless. Now Sam absolutely had to make sure he was there, to meet Michael, and of course because he wanted to help prepare some of the food and drinks. He went home that night, unable to sleep, and unable to stop smiling. Thanksgiving Day came before he knew it.

Sam sat impatiently in the rocking chair on the snow-covered front porch of Thomas's house sipping on a warm rum apple cider. Guests arrived slowly and Sam got acquainted with everyone. Not too long after about half of the group had arrived, a tiny cerulean blue smart car pulled up to the side of the road and out stepped....him.

Him was the man who Sam had been so eager to meet. Michael Kennington.

The sweet man that Sam had been in correspondence with for the past month was finally here. It felt like so much longer and the wait had been more than worth it.

Michael was not hard to describe: a 6'4 man with a muscular build, and very easy on the eyes. Though he was certainly tall, there wasn't any intimidation and Sam felt nothing but safe and calm.. He had the appearance of a man who could be turned on by something as simple as someone reading a book; his dark rimmed glasses never once moved from his eyes. He was rugged but clean, built but not overly generous; his smile could have made heaven jealous. There was a peculiar mystery about him as well, as if behind closed doors he took his glasses off before using whips, drinking whiskey on the rocks while he fucked you like an animal. But he did not use whips, and he controlled his liquor intake, and in all honesty his sexual tenacity was unknown to Sam but he was not too interested in such things. Sam was immediately turned on by three qualities: his divine smile, his candid simplicity, and his artistic backbone—all three of which enhanced his attractiveness. In just the short month that they had been communicating, Michael had lived up to all of Sam's expectations and much more. Sam was instantaneously star struck and Michael was all he could dream about that night.

In the dream, there was Sam and there was Michael. They were on a dock, not touching, but looking at each other in a peaceful trance, the water lightly chopping at the shore.

"I feel like I've known you for years," Sam began, breaking the porcelain silence.

"How did it feel?" Michael said, an idea forming in his

mind.

"How did what feel?"

"Meeting me. How did it make you feel?"

Sam smiled a sort of smile that already gave away what he had thought and Michael returned the expression.

"How did it make *you* feel?" said Sam, wanting him to start. Michael pondered this smartly and shortly.

"Like we had been past lovers, perhaps on the swim team, and when we would go to swim camp over the weekend, would sneak out of our cabins at night and watch the lunar eclipse together, holding hands, wondering what would happen to us after the week was over."

Sam was surprised at the depth of this response, but was turned on by Michael's articulate flow, and hence, went with the fantasy. Sam continued the story.

"Promising to keep in touch after it was all over, and we were home in our own beds with only postcards and the memory of each other's warm faces to keep us company. We wanted to see each other, we were dying to see each other, but we weren't allowed to. We had to wait another year. Another long, painstakingly drawn out year without so much as a phone number. When we saw each other again, when that moment arrived; we would embrace each other, just like we had before."

"And I would play you my piano recordings on an old cassette tape player and you would get on your knees."

"And I would get down on my knees beside you, beside your welcoming presence, and just listen to the sound of you pouring your magic on those wonderful ivory keys, those keys that had been the conception and birth of so many emotions. But there, in that frame of time, the only emotion we had was happiness—happiness that the lover that was lost was found again and right where he should be. In the company of the one he most cared for."

"And the morning birds," Michael continued, "could be heard trickling out from the black trees above. A lost moon. We bent the truth when Counselor Murphy asked how those dirt tracks managed to make their way into the cabin. We could hardly eat our macaroons served at snack time."

"And in the company of the other boys, chatting away about what bugs they found or what their older brother had told them about how the greatest feeling in the world was a warm wet pussy, we ignored all of this. We just ate our snacks and glanced at each other, with a knowing that that evening we would sneak off again, into the small forest, near the reeds of the lake and sit on the dock, watching the moon casting a dreamlike gleam on the lake and on us. But even if it were not out, we would always have the light in each other's eyes, no matter how dark it got outside." The End.

"Is that how it would all go then?" Michael asked, with a smirk about him. A boat made its way across the small waves, but neither party paid attention to the other. There were more important things happening, for now.

"Yes, that would be perfect." There was a silver mist brushing the water. Some orange leaves fell amongst the deadening ground.

"Perfect is pretty hard to achieve, you know." He said this almost as if he recognized the lie immediately after he said it.

"Not with you," Sam said, convinced.

"Do you mean that?" Michael knew that he did.

"What would you say if I told you I loved you?" Sam blinked, but there was nothing but "…Michael?"

But Michael didn't respond. Instead he was gone, and the words that Sam had just said were whisked away on the wind's wings.

The chilly autumn breeze died down. The waves did the same and the birch trees off in the distance became so surreal, they just looked like they had been painted there. Everything was gone and Sam woke up from the illusion, heart still pounding.

Michael and his overwhelming biceps had accidentally scooted Sam over to the right a little as he had passed out on the air mattress with him last night. Their friend Patrick was beside Michael on the left side. Sam looked around the room and observed everyone else still fast asleep, probably still full from dinner the day before and undoubtedly still a little drunk as well. Sam knew he was, and tried to shake the unwelcome hangover from his head to no avail.

He checked the clock on the wall.

9:15am.

Michael batted his eyes open to see that Sam was awake. Sam turned his head and returned the look, he was still waiting for Michael to answer the question, but he knew that a different Michael in a different time had heard him ask that. This Michael did not know that Sam loved him very much, and just yawned, saying good morning quietly so as not to wake anyone.

"Good morning," Sam replied sweetly.

"Did you have fun yesterday?" Michael said, rubbing his hands over his face.

"Time of my life." There was no need to lie, he truly had.

"I'm glad."

"You?"

"It felt like a dream."

"Want some coffee?" Sam asked, semi blushing for no reason at all.

"I'd love some," and with that Michael kissed Sam on the forehead and that was all Sam needed.

Sam kissed Michael back, also on the forehead, went into the kitchen, a smile growing across his entire face. Thankfully there was a pot already made because he didn't know how to make coffee yet. He grabbed a couple of tiny ceramic mugs. One had a picture of a mountain on it, the other just covered with a simple glaze. He poured the contents of the pot into both. The steam danced from the cups and the aroma hypnotized him. It was like a sister smell of weed. Both entranced, both tasted so good, and both got him high but in different ways.

He brought the cups back into the living room and handed one to Michael.

"Thank you," he said sweetly.

"You're welcome," Sam replied back cordially. "I had a dream about you last night."

"Oh, really? What was the dream about?"

"It was the last day of swim camp and the two of us were standing on the dock. I asked you if you loved me."

"What did I say?"

"You didn't."

"I didn't?"

"I woke up after that."

"Are you still waiting for a response?"

Yes.

"No," Sam lied. He was still waiting, but he knew Michael's feelings differed.

"A different Sam is waiting for that response, Michael. The Sam in front of you is just glad he got to meet you." It wasn't the whole of it, but it was true. He said this, turning the other way to drink his coffee.

"It was so good to have finally met you, Sam."

"I feel the same, Michael."

He pinched himself but he didn't wake up. The whole

night really had happened and he hoped with a golden hope that Michael, deep down inside, felt the exact same way. Before he could blink, the fleeting November morning and the company of Michael Kennington were taken from him.

Times these days were harsh and a recession had been zapping the nation of financial stimulation to ominous levels. The economy was not faring any better for Sam Reed, who had now lived three years of unemployment. The need for cash was imperative for him and he was willing to do just about anything including fast food but luckily none were hiring at the time. He continued to keep in touch with Michael but the two were certainly not together, or even in an open relationship—just friends. For some inner conflicting reason, Sam could not bring himself to sleep with anybody else. He would consider that rude. A slap in the face to the short lived yet wonderful time spent in the innocent, beautiful company that Michael offered. But somewhere down his dark path of assumptions, that conviction wasn't going to hold for much longer.

But I'm here to help you, Sam.

That damn voice was back. (Shut up Will!)

I'm here to make you feel beautiful and loved in a world that wants to mock you and make you feel ugly and unwanted. I'll make all of that go away. I'll make the world respect you. You won't be an addict; you'll be adored, adored by something you can't get from the rest of the world. Don't abdicate yourself from me, Sam. I told you, I know what's best. I know... I know...

He brushed the voice off of his shoulder and told it to shut up and that he wasn't interested.

"You don't know shit about me."

Sam held himself out for a month, and then the ropes

came back and tied him back up to that leather cross of shameful, void-filling, sex. He had wanted it so badly before but now it was like a drug addict picking up the needle again, relinquishing his craving for it, and then crying as he failed to resist letting it get the best of him again. Sam felt as though he had shot up too many times and now as his veins pulsated with the aberrant sensation of his abiding sexuality, those black and blue track marks popped up again like ugly snake tongues. Truth be told, he was in no way, shape or form addicted to sex. The only true addictions Sam had ever had were in his fantasies and storytelling (a more colorful and artistic way of saying compulsive lying). It was like that catchy line they used for Pringles (betcha can't have just one!), couldn't tell just one lie. It was too good, tasted too wonderful, and all the additives and preservatives in them made Sam feel like shit seconds after it happened. Such was the way with lying. But sex was the issue at hand. An addiction, no, but something that was nonetheless desired.

He scanned through a message on the hookup site that he had been on which described an offer for sex; and there was going to be cash paid—something that Sam would readily and easily turn down, but honestly, he wanted money. The greed inside of this man was a nasty kerosene to this idea. Sam tried to find what the rest of him looked like. There was no headshot but he saw a well-defined body and decided to go with it. The man gave him directions to such and such a house and Sam hopped the bus to meet him there that day.

"Just let yourself in, and don't let me know you're here. I want to find you in the bathroom, naked," is what the unflattering message that the man had sent, read.

Sam felt uncomfortable immediately but he ignored the sensation.

"I'll leave the $100 on the bathroom counter for you."

Red Flag. He held his breathe as he typed his response.

"Ok, I'll see you there." His tone was depressing and he was grateful the computer could not convey emotion.

"Wait, what did I just do?"

He had. There was no turning back now.

He was still in his trance of not really understanding what he was doing as he got off the bus and began walking, trying to find where the man lived. There were many houses and the vague description the man kept giving was not helping. Sam looked up as if the answer was drawn in airplane smoke up in the sky, and saw those familiar dark clouds boiling above his head that made the air around him feel downright paranormal. Sam had a very bad feeling about everything before anything had begun.

After almost an hour of highly irritating searching, Sam finally received the text that he was in fact right in front of the house and truth be told he was so irritated that he wasn't even in the mood for sex anymore. Sam was, however, in the mood for money and this is the only thing that forced him from saying to hell with the whole thing because at this point he was very tired and wanted more than anything to just go home. He went around the house to the back door and when he found it unlocked let himself in and found that he was in the bedroom, which was unoccupied. So figuring this whole thing was going down in another part of the house, he moved on and began exploring other parts of the residence. He turned the corner to the bathroom and saw it on the counter as soon as he looked the promised one hundred dollars for his keeping. For a second he thought about just taking the money and running, and thus began trying to justify that action would be far more virtuous than having sex with someone for it, right? The picture that he had been sent to Sam though gave him no cause for hesitation. No sooner had he rounded the corner than a door across the way from which he had came, opened and out walked...him.

.

The next half an hour in that house was an inescapable bad dream. Even though Sam kept his eyes closed the entire time, he knew everything else around him was fuzzy. It was closely compared to being drunk and not having a good time; just feeling sick. There was something that was happening to him that he couldn't explain or stop. It was all a mixture of shock and speechless disgust with himself. Sometimes it felt like he was enjoying it, but he knew he really wasn't. He hated it, this thing that he was doing.

Boxed up in his heart's attic he realized something he hadn't before. It came in incremental torrents. First, with that day in second grade when that girl called him stupid. Then, in middle school when the faggot adjective was a popular Sam synonym; the Andy days when his heart was not broken, just fractured, and even what he went through with Jenny, doing something for the better outcome of someone else, rather than himself. As the saying goes, he was looking for love in all the wrong places; showing it to all the wrong faces.

It felt sacrilegious to be thinking of this right now but in retrospect he was reminded of a story in the Bible of when Jesus asked Peter if he loved him:

"Simon Peter, Son of John. Do you love me more than these?

"Yes, Lord, you know that I love you."

"I ask you again, Simon Peter, Son of John, do you love me?"

"You know all things Lord, and you know that I love you."

"Simon Peter, Son of John, Do you truly love me?"

"I would lay down my life for you, Lord."

Yet even before saying this, Jesus knew Peter would come to deny him three times. Such was the story with Sam and the world. It felt like everybody needed him around for an emotional punching bag but nobody really wanted him.

Do you love me, World? This was always the necessary question.

Of course we love you, Sam. Smiles adorned their faces, fists clenched and ready behind the valleys of their backs.

I ask you again World, do you really love me? I just, need to know for my well-being and trust.

Why do you ask this, Sam? Of course we love you. Plotting grins and unfriendly glances turned his way when he blinked.

Finally, and for the sake of my serenity and clarity, I ask you World, Do you truly love me? A subtle shout of desperation…

We would lay down our lives for you, Sam.

Yet before Sam could even see the sunrise of his first birthday, the world had shown him that it did not hold the love he searched for. It continued to do its damage. It released its Hounds, its Andy's and its Drunken Man. All these things, in the eyes of Sam Reed anyway, had been simply about one thing only. Finding that unequivocal love and acceptance. Not some "hey, will you love me and cherish me forever?" or "hey will you be my friend for a while until you have to go away?" Sam wanted something that few people really want…REAL love, but the bullets never missed when he went looking for it.

It was over almost as quickly as it began, and Sam tried to hide the tears.

He didn't stay for any conversation. He barely even looked at the man. "What's the matter?!" Don't you want to stay for seconds? My boyfriend will be home any minute." The man's laugh was empty.

"I should probably catch the bus home. I need to eat something," Sam said with a hint of sadness in his voice that the other man didn't seem to detect and Sam was grateful for this.

"Ok, call me sometime and maybe we can do this again, same pay, same game?"

"I'll-uh-I'll give you a text," Sam said and without another word he walked to the bathroom, put on his pants and grabbed his things, walking out of the door without even looking back. He waited a few more minutes before the bus came, then boarded it and went on his way home. The bullet was shot, the child left unloved, and the rain of the world continued to fall on the plane of his soul.

It was an uncharacteristic feeling Sam had. He thought that getting paid money for having sex would be a win-win for him but for some reason his heart had sunk to a new level, his body felt disgusting, and he was almost on the verge of hysteric tears. He didn't feel good about himself whatsoever. It wasn't even the fact that the man was disgusting, or that Sam had technically done something illegal, it was just so unexplainable. Knowing that he had given himself away to some stranger for $100 just didn't have the appeal it had when he had first thought of the idea. It had stripped him of any dignity he had left. The sun was still shining just like before except just a little bit cooler. There was no rain anywhere to be found, and he didn't understand why. The bus ride home seemed to take an eternity but Sam didn't care; he needed to be alone with his thoughts. When the bus hit the halfway mark between Lynville and the one he had just came from, it started to drizzle.

"Missed your cue," Sam muttered under his breath. "Could've used you a while ago." He was alone when he arrived at his place. He went to his room and lay on his bed soaking in a great amount of remorse and misery. He joined the rain and wondered if there was any possible chance that he would ever forgive himself for this and he doubted that there was. For the first time in a very long while he looked upward to the ceiling, past the enclosure, towards the place where he thought heaven might be and with the lightest breath and a single tear running down his cheek he quietly let out...

"God, I am so sorry."

For so long now he had wanted change in his life, a break from the ordinary and tormenting lifestyle that he thought had oppressed him. He thought that all these things that he had done so far would bring him that unfailing happiness he was looking for, but instead it had all been a masquerading bravado that had pained him with misery and discontent. Sam admittedly was broken and he needed repair or a different sort of fix. That sort of medicine didn't come in a capsule or a bottle. It came from somewhere else. He was first and foremost a creation of God, whether he wanted to believe it or not. He had put up such a stiff fight because this entire time he had thought that God was the one who had hurt him and abandoned him when in fact it was an ignorant band of misinformed, tyrannical, wannabees who had broken his heart. Not God, who he knew must still love him even if it was on some infinitesimal level. If nobody else loved him, the one who made him surely did. Of course he did, why wouldn't he? He held onto this dwindling, optimistic thought but it turned to dust in a matter of seconds. God didn't...couldn't possibly love him. Maybe that Will character had been right all along, love had just been a scapegoat for tolerance.

"Look's like all you're doin' is returnin' the favor. Touché, Jesus."

When his mother walked into the room and saw him on his bed, she immediately bypassed the thought that something was wrong and just went right up to him asking what it was.

"Mom, if I told you something would you be mad?"

"Depends." Not comforting at all.

He decided to just spit it out, beating around the bush for too long would make him second guess wanting to tell her.

"I'm gay."

Juliet peered into him, to make sure this wasn't some sort of a test.

"Why would you say that?"

"Because that's who I am."

"Well I don't think that's the person God created you to be."

"Well, you're not necessarily someone I would go to get approval for a lifestyle. I just want to know if you still love me."

"Sam, even though I don't agree with that kind of behavior, there is nothing that you could possibly do that will ever make me love you any less."

"Promise?"

"Absolutely."

"I love you," she said to him. Juliet was not smiling and he knew why, but her words were sincere. Sam had not been thrown out of the house and he was grateful that he received some kind of reassurance that he was still loved for who he was. Maybe not fully accepted, but parents just don't readily accept everything. That's what friends are for. Parents are there to tell you they will always love you no matter what and Juliet had told Sam just that.

"I love you, too."

He wiped the smile off his face when she left the room and reminded himself of why he was laying on his bed in the first place.

With those words, he and the rain went inside himself, alone.

December 18, 2010: Ending the Storm

Rain...

That's what there always was, always.

It was there, then it was not, and then it was again.

This time it was there, of course it was.

Had it ever really left?

Samuel Brandon Reed knew the answer to that question but did not know he knew it. He was drifting in and out of the rain, hearing it but not quite acknowledging it. It had a familiar air about it, as if it had badgered this hard before on a different windowpane, trying to get the attention of someone else who had been ignoring it. The ground was saturated and all the plants looked as if they were plastic as they shined, wet. Flowers hung low, and the trees even stooped, not as upright as they should be. It was full-blown misery outside, and inside.

He lay on his bed soaked with the nausea of his diminished pride and deteriorating optimism with the certainty that this was, of course, a regretful decision he would try to get over in time, but uncertain as to whether or not he would ever forget that he had done it. He didn't think that he ever would. He had passed the level of childlike curiosity and entered into the threshold of transgression meets desperation. Sam knew what it was to unabashedly relish in the sweet stench of heavy sin. He was now left in the wreckage and the waste of his decisions. He scolded himself over and over again until he was sick of it. Then he scolded himself some more. It was one week until Christmas and there was not a flake of snow predicted in the forecast.

I'm a whore, he thought to himself. He repeated this again and the truth of it rang ferociously outward and then came quietly home to him.

No, not a whore, maybe just a little sexually enthusiastic. The little voice inside of him tried to pipe up but it was silenced almost immediately. There was no justifying what he had done.

"This isn't me," he said to himself, "this isn't how Sam Reed was raised."

This wasn't entirely true but Sam was missing one major point. There was more than one person responsible for his raising. His mother had nurtured him, cleaned up after him, and taught him right from wrong. From there on, there was only so much a mother could do. For the most part, any sort of learning disability or ADHD aside, Sam knew what he was doing when he was doing it. He had put his faith on the back burner and allowed a devil in through the doggy door. He picked up his own bottles of booze and drank them all by himself. No one had ever forced him to do this, but he wanted to be seen as a child no longer, However, this longing had crossed the line and even though Sam had never been the best at distinguishing where such lines were drawn, he saw this as clear as day.

He had finally arrived, destination reached.

He had become the person he feared most, and as much as it killed him to admit it he was without a doubt now, the demon, as he had been this whole time now without even realizing it. He had been the hound chasing him in his nightmares, it was he who had been the darkness lurking at the edge of his bed as a child, and he had been the monster that kept him from falling asleep at night. He had even been the disease that had ravaged him so terribly. And now, lying in his bed, he was the child again, realizing that the monster existed and wondering when it would strike next. Upsetting still was how much he really didn't feel a thing when he thought of this. Nothing was a surprise anymore; it was all just a disgusting realization. The blood red dress he had once imagined wearing was ripped at the seams, revealing his fishnet leggings. The lipstick smudged across his lower mouth. Mascara ran down the side of his face and the heat of the spotlight had turned cold and red. He felt like Carrie White, that poor little girl that had been so misunderstood by everyone now covered in pig's blood and the center of attention in front her class "mates" but for all the wrong reasons. He could almost hear Carrie's mom in the background yelling at him directly.

"They're all gonna laugh at you! They're all gonna laugh at you!"

They already were.

That's exactly what the voices in his head were doing. Over and over until his ears felt like they were going to bleed. Even sounds and voices that he had never heard before were just created in the chasms of his head for the sole purpose of pitiful self-torment.

He pondered all these things in the sanctuary of his room, tears welling up inside of him as he did so. Responsibly entering back into the reality, he did what he had always done in times such as these; he pulled out a notebook and a pencil from the drawer beside his bed. He looked at the pencil as though it were a forgotten friend.

"Hey there comrade, dearest, sweet comrade of mine. Got any bullets left old buddy? Need to shoot me up some bad guys, need to shoot 'em up til' they're good and dead on this here loose-leaf. You're all I got, partner. I can count on you can't I? Of course I can, you've always been there and you always will be. Of course you will; you won't disparage me, will ya? Course you won't. So do you think you can you help me out here? Can you help a heartless fellow out?"

Sam stared at the blank page and it stared right back. It was a bare stare, with no mocking air about it, but if anything, pure untainted sympathy. With every word and emotion there, ever was available to him at that moment, and he was feeling the vast majority of them, he could write nothing,

Not one damned word.

The will was more than just there. It was wanting and waiting to be given the green light, but the inspiration and the ignition point was nowhere in sight nor mind. Everything raced around in his head like a horse track where it all ended up going everywhere but where he wanted it to go most of all. Thoughts, words, ideas were all animals running wild, unable to be caged and tamed. In usual situations of writer's block, Sam would simply walk away and come back when ideas had calmed down and matured. But for some reason, this time, this story had to be released right now at this moment before it was lost. He started at square one, with no story, but with a poem that he used as a springboard into the unknown.

There used to be a point in my life
Where I could stay far above the ground and fly
That was on a much different cloud

A cloud of childhood where flying was possible
Now in this thunderhead of dismal adult disarray
I hover over what was once my existence
And watch it get struck with lightning
Over and over
And battered with hailstones
Over and over
I find it easy to gravitate towards wrong
So hard to find the medium of right
I'm on a balance beam of good and bad.
When I board, I choke, and I instantly fall off
And fall to the earth below, shattering into many pieces
My childhood watching me, remembering me, crying
Wondering what led itself to crumble and decay
I could never be up in the sky
I was never meant to fly, only to cry and
Watch my sorry little life pass me right the fuck by.

He crumpled it up, intending to throw in it the trashcan but just tossed it across to the other side of the room instead and sat back down on the bed, arms folded.

Music faded in and out of his ears but he hardly noticed it. Notes and melody of all the right kind pounded at the door of his brain trying to get in but he wasn't answering them. He was just lying there with a pointless and obsolete feeling like he had been chasing after the wind his entire life, those hailstones and lightning bolts still badgering him, just like that rain had done with Juliet. Now it was Sam's turn to know what this felt like. He just felt as though he needed to get on a soapbox, hold up his megaphone and scream to the world his transgressions, but it would do him no good. They would do what they always did: point, laugh, and judge. They knew how to do these things better than anyone else, but there was always his music—something that could not point, could not judge, could not hurt him. It could only calm his mind and make the poison a little less present, and that's when he turned up the song. He heard the piano chime four times, his mind chimed soon after. It was peculiar how it all went. "All These Things that I've Done," was a song Sam had heard so many times before, but it entered his ears as though he was hearing it for the first time as though the song had new meaning, because this time, it did. He opened his ears and his mind and the band seemed to be whispering only to him.

When there's nowhere else to run.

There wasn't, he saw none, he was trapped. He saw the hound, he saw himself, the beast was running to catch him again, his knife-like fangs barreling in.

Is there room for one more, sun?

There was no room for any more Sams in here. Christ, didn't he have enough masks already. No room, No room!

One more sun.

One more? Or just one, period? I can't really decide on one right now, I'll have to get back to you.

If you can hold on.

Tryin' to, but the rains in the way, just rainin' like mad in here right now.

If you can, hold on.

Almost slipped, no, saved myself, just barely.

Hold on.

He had to hold on…he could do it, he knew he had to.

There is something that happens to a person when they re-examine their life, something unseen on the surface. They become something else. They reject everything up to this point that has told them they were going to fail. To see nothing but the light and that beautiful place that life has brought them to. For Sam he was finally realizing that it gets better. And then he had it, by God, by the sweet blessed power of Christ himself he had it, and it flowed like the Danube out of his head and through his hand, onto those wonderful pages of paper. This was exactly what he needed to say and what everyone around him needed to hear once and for all, which was simply the truth: the whole truth, the truth that he had hidden but wanted to hide no longer.

I wanna stand up.
Despite my crippled state.

I wanna let go.
Let go of everything.

You know, you know, no you don't, you don't.
You already do, I've told you.

I wanna shine on, in the hearts of men.
The real me, the ME me, why don't I shine? Who do I shine for?

I wanna meet them from the back of my broken hand.
From the back of course, can't see me broken, nope, never gonna see it again.

Another head aches.
From the lies.

Another heart breaks.
Same old reason.

I'm so much older than I can take.
So true, what the hell happened to me? Where'd the time go?

And my affection, well it comes and goes.
This time it was staying, for my sake let's hope.

I need direction to perfection no, no, no, no help me out!
But, perfection wasn't reachable, only the rain was. Still needing some of that help, though.

Yeah yeah you know you've gotta help me out.
Yeah oh don't you put me on the back burner.
Who was going to help me out? I don't think anyone will this time around, back to square one again. No one wanted to help me. I *was* the back burner this time; no one wanted me no more.

And when there's no where else to run.
Lies, it was such a lie. Sam thought there had to be a place to run, someone to help him run there, someone who could show him how amazing life could really be. He felt as though he had been in the gutter for so long that the rain had become trivial and the sunshine just wasn't something he knew how to see anymore.

Is there room for one more sun?

And then it hit him; it hit him as if the fist of Zeus had turned into the world's biggest wake up call. As though every great realization that man himself had ever thought, flew down from heaven and back up from hell, converging into one majestic epiphany beating him down to the ground like a massive welcomed thunderbolt of revelation.

He found a place to run.

There was room for one more chance, One more Sam...he was it, but was it all really this simple? It couldn't be, but there it was as plain as day, as plain as the sun.

Sam was the help he had needed all along. He had been the rain, this whole time, it wasn't anything or anybody else, but him. He himself brought the storms. The thought was almost hilarious, why hadn't he seen this sooner? Through all of the misery, through every heartbreak, every time a gun to the head felt like the only excusable way out of anguish, he could have been there for himself. Sam Reed was his own worst enemy. He was Lee, he was the hound, he was the person he had never wanted to become, someone who was afraid of so much that he had begun to be afraid of his own damn shadow. All he had ever needed to do was just simply believe that he was good enough and the rain would have stopped. The sun would have come out and the light would have been permanent, but being the blinded individual that Sam was this hadn't happened. He had lied to himself that it had. But the truth was, this was the first time that he had sincerely seen himself as someone of worth.

Right there.

In that moment.

These changes, ain't changing me,

They already had though, somehow or another, with or without his permission, they had changed everything about him. Some of it was lovely, some of it was not.

The gold-hearted boy I used to be.

Used to be? This line puzzled him for a minute.

What happened to me? He thought to himself. I used to be the epitome of everything I had ever wanted to be. I had been the upstanding person that knew no wrong. How had he let himself fall to such depths?

Everyone has a price.

The words reverberated fiercely in his mind and as heartbreaking as it was for Sam to admit that, and it was, he too had his price. It was the undeniable truth. But what did Sam know of truth? He was a compulsive liar, for Christ's sake. He didn't know what truth was. He wouldn't know it if it hit him in the face.

Yeah, yeah you know you've gotta help me out.

You've got to help me, God; I might not be able to do this one without you.

Yeah, yeah oh don't you put me on the back burner.

Not like the way I put *you* on the back burner, so easily, so easily.

You know you've gotta help me out.

Won't ask any more favors.

Yeah, you're gonna bring yourself down.

Already have, so easily. I didn't do it all by myself this time, I did have some assistance. Some people out in the audience that I would like to congratulate.

Yeah, you're gonna bring yourself down.

I've already brought myself down. To the depths, I tell ya. I can think about is my own soul, do I even have a soul? I'm sure I do.

I've got soul but I'm not a soldier.

Seem to be the only who does anymore.

I've got soul but I'm not a soldier.

I have it, somewhere, just gotta find the sucker.

I've got soul but I'm not a soldier.

So much soul, so little soul at the same time.

I've got soul but I'm not a soldier.

But what?

I've got soul but I'm not a soldier.

Of course you aren't, your battle is of a different kind my friend.

I've got soul but I'm not a soldier.

I'm not; I'm just not, not. Me, not ever.

I've got soul but I'm not a soldier.

I'm a hundred of them? All fighting for attention.

Time.

To set things right?

Truth.

Be told, not sure that there is *any* truth left in here.

Hearts.

I got myself a whole canister of them, so every time that one breaks, I can just grab me a new one, put it inside of my chest, and keep on going. I have to keep going, there's nothing to stop this now, I have it all and it's in these pages.

Over and in.

Over the rain, and in the sunshine now.

Last call for sin.

I'd love to take another shot but you see I just can't, gotta get out of this here rain before I drown.

While everyone's lost.

Nobody else lost, it was all a lie. They're all just waiting for me to make the first move so I can lose…lost so much already I fear there just ain't nothing else left to lose.

The battle is won.

But that was the truth, it was. Even Sam had won.

With…

…It dawned on him that it was because he was not just listening to it anymore, he understood it. Understanding opened the floodgates and those words, oh heavenly words, emptied out onto the bare page like rain on desiccated, desert dirt as the faultless lines reverberated so sweetly. Sam recalled it all, from bliss to scorn, disgrace and drugs, innocence and sex, lies and apologies, sunshine, and rain. He thought of the ridicule and both the strength and weakness derived from it. He thought of the love he had given and received and how funny it was how equal the two really were. Nothing was left out, every memory flowed free and it did so with ease. Sam knew this was what was right, for it would not have been so easy was it not.

As he wrote the story of his life; withholding no event; that badgering rain finally stopped hitting the window. The harsh howl of the wind died and a beam of sunlight made its way through the window and lit up the poet's changed face. He was no longer in darkness, not anymore. It was finally possible to find the sunlight amidst the storm and as he so wonderfully observed now, there was much more joy to behold than there were sufferings to hold on to. Sam knew that all these things had been there, that this storm had ravaged him for a remarkable reason, because the sunshine was that much brighter when the clouds were gone, and they were. They really were. The storm outside had ended and moved on. Drops of water fell off of plants and trees and onto the soil and everything smelled so crisp and new. The sun's luster seared the ground and steam rose from the wet concrete back to the sky where it would return to the clouds and start again, falling back down as rain somewhere else. That was the way it changed, that was how it started over. Sam, however, wasn't aware that any of this was going on, because he was, once again, elsewhere.

He was also changing.

He was starting over himself.

He had fallen, now he was rising again, back into the

clouds, although this time he would not fall to the ground again. There were going to be no more cuts on his wrist or bruises on his eye. It would be different; this time. He would remain aloft among angels and though he continually glanced up in the sky, not knowing *what* was up there looking down at him, one way or another, that's where he knew he would be, happy as he could be.

As Sam lay on his bed soaking in and writing about all these things that he had done, he felt the start of something much more magnificent than what his pre-conceived notion of happiness had been. Much, much greater.

He felt a power unknown to him for these last twenty-two years. It was the power of change, and not just a change for himself but for everything and everyone around him.

And with that powerful light, he was intent on doing marvelous things.

The words his mother had whispered in his ears those many years ago rang out multitudes of glorious and overdue truths. He dreamily lifted his head from his paper, smiling and crying at the same time. Teardrops stained the pages, hitting the ink and gushing it outward in little streams. He was overcome with a joy that he shouted out to himself by whispering to the world:

"Everything *will* be alright."

That was the quintessential truth, and he knew it now more than ever, so very well indeed. That this luminous holy shine was not seeable without the blood and the darkness that he had, for so many years, been crowded by. That this breed of happiness could not have come without lethal heartbreak, and that this change, this long, overdue metamorphosis that he was undergoing would never have been attained without the sweet and sour antidote that was the surrounding presence of...

"All these things that I've done."

All these things that he had done.

Sam Reed looked upward once again at the bright sky. This time he willingly and humbly set down his shaking fists, with a salty sincerity in his tears, smiled, and said thank you.

♦ ♦ ♦

This book was begun on December 18, 2010 and was completed October 1, 2011.

And with the gentlest hands,

Now my tale is finally told.

Epilogue:
After the Storm

In case you are still concerned about some of the people in this book and where Sam's relationship with them stands, here is your update.

Jenny made a 100% recovery from her ordeal with drugs and alcohol and has been clean and sober now for about a year. She recently got her first job since she got back from rehab in California, but lost her mom to a heart attack about a year later. Through all of this they remain the best of friends and he could not be prouder of her and the remarkable woman she is becoming.

Abigail and Sam recently had coffee before she moved to Idaho with her family and her mother greeted him with an enormous hug. It probably helped that he did not wet himself this time. She herself is quite a writer and they send each other poems and stories that they have written. They consider each other very close and dear friends.

Michael and Sam are still in very close communication, but due to their distance and the fact that neither of them drives, they don't get to see each other. On the subject of whether Michael told Sam if he loves him yet or not. I am letting that take its own course and we continue to deeply encourage each other in our art: him in his videographing, Sam in his writing. They plan on collaborating on a few projects sometime in the near future.

As for Sam Reed…he never went back on medication and life for him could not be better. He continues to hold hope for the Christian faith and that there are some good people out there who aren't just about destroying you in order to make you something else. Sam's head is continued to be held up towards God or whoever is out in that never-ending universe with an optimistic chin that they have something even better planned ahead. Sam is, and always will be, a proud member of the GLBT community and is out to show the world that love knows no bounds, physically or spiritually.

I am truly a changed person for the better because of this book.

Thank you,
Tyler Reedus

About The Author

Tyler Reedus is a Washingtonian to the core—rooted in the Northwest, but with an appreciation for foreign cultures. He enjoys creating and reciting poetry, and always finds weather, especially rain, to be one of his greatest inspirations. A movie buff, Tyler prefers film that's full of vivid, detailed, high-octane drama and writes in this same vein: he likes to keep people's fingernails digging into their armchairs.

Still in his early twenties, Tyler delivers the result of a life uncorked prematurely—and what's come out is his own epic memoir. He promises the raw emotion upon these pages will rattle readers, in a very good way.

All These Things is his first novel.

www.ingramcontent.com/pod-product-compliance
Lightning Source LLC
Chambersburg PA
CBHW020317260626
47156CB00004B/1254